SHADOWS OF SOLSTICE

BONNIE ELIZABETH

My Big Fat Orange Cat Publishing

Shadows of Solstice
My Big Fat Orange Cat
Fiction February 2021

My Big Fat Orange Cat Publishing
MyBigFatOrangeCat.com

ISBN 978-1-953363-04-6 trade paperback

Chapter One

Sometimes there's a reason for superstitions. Like legends, there can be kernels of truth hidden in amongst the tales. Festivals, particularly religious festivals are often shrouded in rituals that few people today understand the meaning of. And yet, to ignore such festivals can mean asking for punishment from a displeased god who won't be ignored.

I believe that's exactly what happened at Havestad Lutheran College in—where else?—Havestad, Minnesota. You probably haven't heard of it. No one has. I hadn't, not until I was being packed off to the college due to my disciplinary probation status at Sankta Lucia University in Dubuque. Something about peddling drugs that were put in the St. Lucia Day buns a club sold at the craft fair my sophomore year.

Like I'm supposed to police what people do with their drugs. It was so unfair. But so was getting kicked out of Pacific Lutheran University. You can see a pattern here? Clearly, my family thought I needed to go to a Lutheran school in order to… I have no idea what it was supposed to do because a Lutheran school isn't exactly like going to boot camp or anything.

But my folks were set upon the whole Mina Andresen will go to a Lutheran college or university and get her degree in business and come home to work with Mom at the family business. A business I had no interest in. I do not want to work in property management or the spin-off idea Mom thought would be great for me. Property staging. Ugh.

Of course, after a few days in Havestad, I was longing for the relative comfort and warmth of my home down in Lake Geneva, Wisconsin. Believe me, comfort and warmth are not exactly the way I normally describe my home, but Havestad is north of Duluth. I didn't even know there *was* anything north of Duluth except maybe Canada and the Arctic Circle.

I have to admit that I might be pushing it if I say that Havestad is "anything." I mean it's slightly bigger than Two Harbors, Minnesota, but that's only because the college fills out the town population.

This was the idea when my family went searching for a school to send me to. They wanted something that wasn't close to a big city. Okay, Duluth is barely an hour away, but in winter the highway isn't the sort of place you want to be driving on regularly if you can avoid it. My car isn't exactly brand new, doesn't have all-wheel drive, and has so many lights glowing on the dash that I worry it's going to come to a halt somewhere along a stretch of highway and I'll end up stuck in some town worthy of a Stephen King novel.

Two Harbors caters to a certain type of tourist with a Burger King, a Comfort Inn, and other big name places around. Lots of hiking and scenery for folks who don't mind a chillier climate while vacationing. I can't say it's relaxing if you're going to spend your time hiking and possibly fishing, though others might disagree.

Havestad is further north and touristy, but in a different way. At some point, the town council had this brilliant idea to make it a cute little movie-ready Scandinavian town with gingerbread trim on the shops and no big name restaurant chains within the city limits. The grocery store was off the main street though it, too, was dressed in pretty colored Scandinavian wood finery.

While Havestad might be hopping in the summer, while school was in session, I can't say the word hopping was appropriate. Chilly, gray days where you feel an uncomfortable nip of cold on your nose starting in October keeps a lot of the tourists at home. Christmas attracts more people, but they're mostly from states further south where snow in December is less common.

From the first of November, wreaths begin decorating doors. By the middle of November, street lamps have ribbons and bows and the lights start going up on the shops, mostly multicolored twinkle lights. At some point, a tree appears.

Through all this, as a student, I'm supposed to be studying and going on about my business while trying to keep the radiator in my room from overheating me and my roommate or freezing us out.

Saturday before finals is the college's Lucia Bride Ceremony. I had heard of the festival at PLU, but managed to ignore it. I apparently helped out one of the campus groups at Sankta Lucia University when I was there by selling them a bit of this and a bit of that to add to their special yeasty buns to make them very special.

No Lucia Bride for St. Lucy's that year. Oops. My bad. Or not. It's not like I knew they were going to sell to the public. I thought it was, like, for a dorm party or something.

Considering each place I got kicked out of had me ending up in a worse place—face it, Tacoma may not be great, but the weather is stunning compared to the Midwest. Yeah, it rains, but it's not so cold. Give me rain and clouds any day over the chill of winter.

Dubuque may not be anyone's idea of fun, but at least there's a city there, uninspiring though I found it.

Now, here I was up on the North Shore and I got clouds, more clouds, winter, and isolation. Go me.

I can't imagine a worse place, but I'm sure if the fifth level of hell appears on Earth my parents will find an appropriate Lutheran school there and send me to it. And because I am not independently wealthy and am disinclined to find a job just yet, I had to go where they sent me. There was also the threat of being disinherited. The family might not be rich, but I expect to get something for the years I had to put up with my mom hovering over me and my dad scolding me regularly about stupid things like a bit of pot and staying out all night.

So there I was, living in an old, crumbly dorm in Havestad, being told I was lucky to have a window that faced the lake, though you couldn't see it for the trees. Still, I'd done fairly well that semester.

I was counting on a solid B from economics. I might even squeak out an A in my business law class. There's an irony there if I ever heard one, but apparently, all the practice I'd had in breaking laws was coming in handy. I had to do well on the final though, otherwise, it'd probably be a B as well. I could pass even if I blew off the final entirely, but I'd never had an A and I was kind of hoping for one.

Like most students preparing for finals, the Lucia Bride festival wasn't really something I was ecstatic about.

"I'm going down to the little fair they have in town," my roommate, Jen said that morning.

It was only nine, earlier than I'm usually up on the weekend, but I wanted to go over everything I needed to study for, or at least economics, which was the final that fell on Monday.

Jen was standing near the closet in our room. I had been stuck in one of the corner rooms, which are odd-shaped things with closets that stuck out of the wall like a wardrobe, giving us a narrow sort of entry hall. Dressers lined the wall closest to the main part of the room and we had just enough space for a small refrigerator and a little microwave on a cart on one side and a loveseat on the other. Our desks sat next to each other across the way, facing a window. A five-foot-high room divider with shelves on either side of it gave us each a bit of privacy and a place for books and other crap. Our beds were tucked off into their separate wings, a narrow little hall just long enough for a twin bed and a walk space next to it. This was the joy of the back corner room. I heard that the room in this spot on the fifth floor had ceilings that angled down and if you didn't walk close enough to the bed, you'd hit your head.

Rumor had it, a girl had knocked herself out.

The wardrobes and drawers had clearly been built into the walls around 1970 with their shiny finished pine wood. The floors had been updated this century and the white computer desks were probably turn of the century things with a few drawers and a pullout shelf for a keyboard.

The building is old enough that the rooms always smell old, that sort of musty smell that seems to get into the very bones of the place and doesn't leave. It also had a hint of something like rosemary in the background, but I could never quite place it. It wasn't a cleanser smell—that was bleach or chemical. This was like a memory of an herb that might have been hung in the building some time long ago.

The radiator between my bed and the desk clicked on with a harsh clank and snort. I always expected puffs of mist to come floating out, but none ever did.

The icy gray skies outside didn't look promising. The grayness made the dark pine of the trees looked nearly black. Safety lamps placed strategically around campus glowed yellow in the morning gloom. A perfect day for studying, because who'd want to do anything else?

If my life wasn't riding on staying in school and graduating, I'd be doing serious drugs. More serious than those I did in Dubuque which I had thought was the near edge of hell. Havestad was one stop closer.

"Looks cold," I said.

Jen laughed. "It's always cold. Get used to it. The best stuff is always out in the morning. We can get stop at the Moo for coffee."

That drew me. The cafeteria coffee had to be made by someone who had never drank a cup in their life. Either that or they hated students with a passion. Jen had a Keurig, but I only had the K cups I could purchase at the local grocery store. The selection was limited. My parents didn't trust me with a credit card so I couldn't order any online.

The Moo was short for Moo and Brew, the local coffee shop. They sold ice cream in the summer as well as coffee. Ice cream sales weren't popular enough for them to stay open in the afternoon in winter, though I had a feeling that as this was a festival weekend, they'd make an exception. It seems they did for certain holidays.

"I'm always up for coffee," I said. I pulled out my winter boots, not because there was snow on the ground, but because they kept my feet warm. I had on socks so heavy I had to twist my feet just so to force them into my boots.

Jen waited, hands in her pockets. She always looked fashionable and today was no exception with her dark black boots, skinny fleece-lined jeans, and a cream turtleneck with candy canes on the neck. Her heavy jacket was unzipped and came down to her hips.

I am always amazed at how blue her eyes are. Her hair is almost black and she swears it's natural despite her fair skin that burns easily in the sunshine. It's one reason she's pleased enough to be in Havestad. There's so little sun she doesn't have to worry that much.

I, on the other hand, don't burn easily. I have lighter hair, though not blonde, and brown eyes, and I could lay out on the beach in Florida all day and maybe get lightly pink. I'm lucky, I know. I'd love to test out my luck on a regular basis someplace warm, but at the rate I'm going, it won't happen until I'm too old to enjoy it. Of course, at least then I won't worry about wrinkles because I'll already have so many a couple of more won't count.

"Ready," I said, pulling my heavy blue and gray coat out of the closet. Mine fell to just below my butt. I was hoping for a long knee-length coat for Christmas because my legs, even clad in long underwear and blue jeans, got cold on days like today.

Jen smiled and we hurried out. Across the hall, our neighbor, Kennedy, waved shyly at us as she returned from the bathroom, the narrow plank pine floor squeaking like an army of mice. Kennedy isn't exactly shy, but she's quiet. She was still in her Wizard of Oz nightshirt over her flying monkey leggings. Naturally, she had on fuzzy red slippers. Kennedy has a thing for *The Wizard of Oz.*

Jen and I hurried past her with Jen just saying, "Moo," which told Kennedy all she needed to know. This has to be the only school where you can moo at another woman and she doesn't get mad.

The walls of our hall were paneled halfway up with shiny cream paint above. At one time, I'd heard there was wallpaper. Now, at least the cream paint kept the hall from being completely gloomy though it did remind me of a horror movie set when I wandered out to use the toilet late at night.

As if my thoughts brought it, I heard a toilet flush in the floor's large communal bathroom. A shower started moments later. I didn't hear anyone yell "flush" so chances were there was only one person in there. The building is so old that if you flush the toilet, it uses all the cold water and the person in the shower will get scalded.

You'd think with all the updates they had to do to get internet connected throughout the place and keep the electrical modernized to handle today's computer equipment that they could have updated the plumbing, too. But perhaps scalding girls in a shower isn't considered too much of a problem for the school.

Five other women were already in the main floor lounge. Two were clearly dressed to go outside, waiting for companions. Jen and I waved. It always pays to be friendly.

The large double doors to the front were stained a darker wood than the floor and held clear stained glass that formed an angel. The lead between the glass was heavy and had darkened from silver to black with flecks of bronze. Gray light played on the floor in front of us. A shadow moved in front of the door, probably a student.

However, when Jen and I exited the building, the only

people were far across the gray cobbled court, too far to have caused a shadow. I shivered in the sudden cold. It could have been a premonition, but back then I didn't believe in such things any more than I believed in superstitions.

Chapter Two

The college is about half a mile from the main street. My dorm room is on the north side of the campus so it's a bit further, requiring us to walk along cobbled paths that wind around various cedars that seem to grow up randomly on the campus grounds. I'm sure someone thought it was picturesque. I think it makes the campus look like nature is taking back the campus a decade after an apocalypse.

The gray skies that are so common here don't help.

I ought to be used to grayness. I lived in Tacoma for a year. But those skies didn't hold the same threat of disaster that these did. Maybe it's looking out at the grayness and knowing it's cold. The air even smelled cold. I can't describe it better than that.

Jen walked across campus quickly, but not in a hurry. She smiled at other students who made their way back from the cafeteria towards the dorms. There were three dorms near ours. Ours was the oldest. Some people, like Jen, liked the quirkiness of the older building and the fact that it was supposed to be haunted. Others preferred the newer dorms with smaller, but more normal-sized rooms that had floors that didn't slope and bathrooms where you didn't have to yell "flush" warning the people in the shower that you were flushing the toilet.

The men's dorms were on the south side of campus. Only two of those, both larger than our four. Havestad wasn't taking any chances that there'd be fraternizing of the sexes. Other Lutheran schools had coed dorms, but not Havestad. That was another selling point for my parents. Not that it mattered to me. I wasn't interested in hooking up with some uptight church boy, and the rebels always find me no matter where I am.

Jen led us to Trinity Lane which goes past the Lutheran Church, a weirdly rounded building that looked mid-century modern with wood sides, stone trim and lots of windows. The rather pointed rounded roof looked a bit like a flattened witch's hat, only in reddish-brown so it blended into the trees.

I'd never been inside as church is not my thing. Cars were parked in the parking lot on the town side of the building. No doubt people were there to get the church ready for the Lucia Bride Ceremony later on.

A block later we entered the actual town. Two older homes, brick and wood bungalows, sat facing each other across Trinity, a short block before you got to the main road. One was a quilt shop. The other remained a residence.

Next to the quilt shop was an old feed store that looked like a large concrete block of a building. On our side of the street was the liquor store and a gas station, complete with convenience store, sitting on the corner of the main street, which was also the highway.

Trinity ended at the highway. Havestad sits up on a cliff overlooking Lake Superior. The buildings across the way backed onto the steep drop that was probably the height of a three-story building.

Jen and I cut through the gas station lot and we were faced with the side of one of the main street buildings, all painted with blue and red flowers beneath gables. The building across the street even had a fake white balcony with gingerbread trim.

The sidewalks were already fairly full, with people wandering around, pausing at vendor booths to look at their wares. Parents held the hands of young children. Cars went by in a steady stream, if not a logjam of vehicles. On non-festival days it's not unusual to see no cars in the time it takes to walk to the Moo.

The Moo is on the campus side of the street, just beyond the corner building which houses a restaurant that serves all sorts of Scandinavian dishes. If someone gets a sweet craving, the restaurant is definitely the place to go. They also serve a good burger and sandwiches. Down the way is the fancy restaurant that serves seafood, lamb, and even, supposedly, reindeer.

The Moo doesn't serve much in the way of pastries, though they do have bagels until they run out. They serve coffees, teas, and in the afternoon, if they're open, ice cream. It's a long narrow room with pictures of cows grazing on green lawns and a few of cows huddling inside a barn with snow outside. Old-fashioned milking equipment is placed artistically next to the walls.

A handful of fifties-style tables with cracked vinyl chairs leaning awkwardly on silver legs sit between the main aisle and the walls. The only windows are those in front. The line for coffee was nearly to the door, but Jen and I squeezed inside, though the place felt hot after the cold walk.

I woke up a bit at the strong smell of coffee. My

stomach growled when I watched a couple settle at a table to eat their bagels.

"I'll get the coffee and a bagel if you want to snag the table over there," Jen pointed. Someone had just cleared off the oldest of the laminate tables. I pulled out a five to give to Jen. She took it and pushed me away.

I settled in to wait. Most people were carrying hats. A few already had packages that had clearly come from a booth rather than a shop. The bags were mismatched and looked reused and ready for recycle. The items inside all appeared to be handmade.

A few were nicer bags that came from the gift shops that lined the street. All six of them. Six might not seem like many if you live in a city, but in a town the size of Havestad, it was more than enough. Most of them held kitschy Scandinavian themed things, though one on the end held expensive wool sweaters.

I could tell the people who had driven here for the festival. They were wearing fancier slacks and nicer sweaters under heavy coats. The locals were all in jeans with older, more worn sweaters, though many were holiday-themed, under their jackets. Some, like me, were just wearing sweatshirts, though mine was an old Sankta Lucia University sweatshirt I had purchased before it became apparent that I'd have to leave.

Jen settled in with our coffees. She dropped change on the table. Neither of us were well-off, though I suspect I was better set than her family, and change made a difference. While we weren't bosom buddies, we were friendly and I could have done far worse in roommates. My freshman year, I'd roomed with another freshman who practically walked with a stick up her ass and found it horrifying that I drank, much less did a few drugs.

I took a sip of my latte, the creamy feel of it in my

mouth and the slightly bitter taste of beans. We each had a bagel as well, slathered with cream cheese. We ate in silence, the conversations swirling around us. I'd about dusted off the crumbs of the bagel from my sweatshirt when a woman came in and started screaming about the church being on fire.

The noise level rose suddenly. People hurried out to the street to see. The way people moved, you'd think the Moo was on fire. Jen and I looked at each other.

"We should go see," Jen said.

I shrugged, getting up. I didn't want to admit that I was as curious about the church as everyone else. It didn't seem in character that I should care about a church. Oddly, I did. The church had become part of my existence in Havestad. Our dorm wasn't super far, but I couldn't imagine that a fire would burn through the campus, the oddly placed trees that towered over the grounds notwithstanding.

The only person still in the Moo, other than the baristas, was an older guy, waiting on a fancy coffee. He was looking behind him as if worried he'd be trapped in the building if he didn't hurry, but clearly didn't want to miss his drink.

Jen and I took our coffees, served in heavy paper to-go cups, and hurried out after the rest of the crowds. Already the air smelled of smoke rather than the pine and chill of the earlier morning. Vendors who didn't want to leave their sidewalk tables were craning their necks. Cars were stopped up at the corner of Trinity.

I heard sirens. The fire department, fortunately, was not on the main street and they were able to take a back-street to the church. Considering the back up on the main road now that people were stopping to look at the smoke, I doubt the trucks would have gotten through.

Jen and I pushed our way through to the corner where a crowd had gathered. It was bigger than anything I'd encountered in Havestad so far. Of course, half the town was out and visitors had come from miles around to see the festival, which, if the flames that began shooting out the side of the church window closest to the parking lot were any indication, wasn't happening that evening.

Someone chuckled in the crowd. I glanced around. Everyone else was focused on the church. No one seemed to be laughing. I wasn't sure where the sound had come from, but it sent a chill down my back.

Standing on the corner watching the flames dance, I couldn't help but feel as if I was waiting for something, though I couldn't have said what.

Chapter Three

I wasted most of the day enthralled by the unfolding disaster. It wasn't so much that I wanted to see the church burn as I was intrigued to see the process the fire department went through to put out the fire. Even as the flames were smothered, people hung around watching. An older woman sat in the parking lot near a car and cried as if she'd lost someone she loved. I worried she had for an hour or so until rumors floated around that there had been no deaths.

I'd learn later that those rumors were wrong, but at that point, they made me feel better.

I heard that the church secretary had suffered from smoke inhalation. Rumor said the pastor had been taken to the hospital with her. Both had been saving a few things from the vestry and altar.

Jen and I listened, along with a crowd of students who had heard the sirens or heard about the fire later on, to people discussing how the fire had started. No one was certain.

One theory was that someone had lit a candle testing

how easy it was to light and it had fallen over and started the pine boughs decorating the church on fire. Someone else heard that it was electrical. The fire department wasn't saying anything, though several of our female students tried their wiles on the men. One of our young men tried to get information from the only woman firefighter in the bunch. She wasn't any more talkative than the men.

Contrary to popular belief, our firefighters were not all that hunky. Just another strike against Havestad.

By the time the sun was going down, my stomach growled and I headed over towards the cafeteria. Jen remained at the church. She has a bunch of friends who are members of the Scandinavian Folk Dance troop. They perform during the Lucia Bride Ceremony and that's a huge big deal, but clearly, without a place for the ceremony, that wouldn't be happening.

As I walked across campus, I had to reflect on the fact that I don't really have friends here. I mean I have people, like my roommate, that I hang with sometimes, and talk to, but I have no one I really look forward to chatting with. Chris, from my business law class, and I study together quite a bit. He's real hunkered down and loves the class so he makes it interesting. I have to say, that his discipline is a huge reason I'm doing as well as I am.

He's the closest person I'd say I have to a friend. Walking across campus in the dusk the idea of being friendless in the cold, chill, northern shore of Minnesota made me sad.

I had almost reached the cafeteria, could actually see the four double doors all open to the outside, the secondary doors still closed to keep out the cold, when Campus Security stopped me.

"Mina Andresen?" the woman asked. She was taller

than I was. Heavyset, too. Her male partner was shorter and quieter, practically buried in his parka.

"Yeah?" I asked. For once I hadn't done anything.

"Come with us." The woman said. I didn't notice a name tag on her jacket. She pushed me around to turn me.

I pulled my arm out of hers. "What's going on?"

"Come with us," the woman repeated. A nametag peeked out. Sandra.

I sighed. If they made me miss dinner, I was going to be pissed. My stomach growled in agreement. I hoped it was loud enough for them to hear.

Campus Security was in the same building as the cafeteria, but it was off to the side with its own entrance down three stairs, making it seem buried. A huge planter hovered around the entrance and no trees towered over it, leaving most sight lines clear.

One place on campus was safe.

I let the quiet guy, Ian, lead the way down the concrete steps. He opened the door and waited for me to go through. Sandra came through last, almost as if she thought I was going to bolt. Granted, I felt like I wanted to, but given that I had no idea what was going on, I had no plans to do so.

Inside, the office was warmer than outside, but not much. The reception area was painted in cream and a long bench was placed near the wall faced by a coffee table. A small reception type window looked out over the area. A young man, a student, sat behind the window.

Ian led me further into the office, through a single white door, and then into a room on the right. A desk sat facing the door and two cheap metal chairs crowded in front of it. Nils Lester sat behind the desk.

I'd met Nils when I transferred to Havestad. I guess my reputation preceded me and the head of campus security wanted to get a good long look at me so he'd know who I was. I'd place Nils in the category of unsatisfied middle-aged man who was just going through the motions. If he were any skinnier he'd be a skeleton. His blonde hair was thin and always looked dull and limp. Not so much greasy as just dull, like it's barely hanging on to life.

In fact, I think Nils looks a bit like that. If he were working at HLC because he couldn't get hired anywhere else I'd understand the look, but from what I'd heard, he'd chosen the place.

"Mina Andresen," Nils said, gesturing at one of the chairs. Sandra and Ian left the room.

The door closed. Sounds of laughter and talking and the occasional shout reached us from the cafeteria. There was an underlying drone of machinery that might have been from the room where the dishes were washed.

"What's up?" I asked. I didn't want to sound too defensive, but I also didn't want to be flip. Jen had been alive and well, surrounded by friends, or at least acquaintances, when I'd left. I'd been with her most of the day.

"I heard part of the reason you're up here at HLC is because of some drugs you put in the food they were selling on St. Lucia Day at your former university," Nils said. He leaned back a bit. If he had a paunch, he'd have crossed his hands over it, but he didn't. Instead, he just had a cream sweater that hung loosely over his frame.

"Maybe," I said. I hadn't ever admitted to the drugs which was why I hadn't been expelled. Instead, because no one could prove anything, I'd been put on disciplinary probation. My folks were the ones who got spooked, worried that Dubuque was too big of a city for me to be part of, and sent me up to Havestad.

And by the way, Dubuque is no one's idea of a big city.

"You have anything to do with that fire at the church?" Nils asked. "Seems you have a problem with Lucia Bride."

My eyes widened. I sputtered and stopped. Whatever I'd been expecting, it hadn't been to be accused of setting a fire. Maybe selling drugs that I hadn't sold on campus, but not that.

"I was with my roommate all day. Not only would I have had no reason to set a fire in the church, I'd not have had the opportunity," I said.

Nils narrowed his eyes at me. "Havestad police are saying it could have been arson. They've asked for a list of students they should watch. You're on that list."

Great.

"You can keep telling me you didn't do it all you like, but you better hope your roommate tells the same tale about being together. They know about you," Nils continued.

Even better.

Not that I was using this year, but if I needed something, no doubt the police would be watching me. The downside of a town this small. Everyone knew everyone else and the chief of police had lived here forever. All they needed to do was say keep an eye on her and the whole town would.

"Didn't do anything," I said. "So I guess there's no need for me to worry."

Nils continued to glare at me, but he didn't stop me from leaving. I wasn't surprised to find a woman in a uniform waiting for me in the reception area. My stomach growled again. Unfortunately, my hunger was just going to have to wait.

Chapter Four

Officer Charla Moline took me down to the Havestad police station about four blocks away. It took longer to follow the short, stocky woman to her car, parked on the edge of campus, let her make a u-turn in the narrow street, and then follow the back roads to the station than it would have to walk directly there.

Of course, it was getting late, and even with my long underwear and heavy coat, it was cold outside. My fingers were numb despite my gloves.

Charla apparently had the shift alone because no one waited in the car for us. I wouldn't have waited in the car with its stink of old cigarette smoke and urine. I tried to imagine how desperate I'd have to be to pee in a car. Couldn't quite do it.

I looked out the window, not touching it with my face because of the various smells and who knew where they were coming from. I did know guys who'd have aimed for the windows if they could, but that was back when I was using and selling a bit.

The police station was a modern building in stone and

wood that stood two stories high, just off the main street. It's around a corner where people can easily find it if need be, but not so visible that it will ruin the fun of the tourists. Even so, it had a peaked roof that rose up wedding-cake-like over both stories. The outside wall planks ran vertical and were painted a bright blue with white trim.

When Officer Moline let me out of the car, I shivered in the cold, though the air was definitely fresher, even with the leftover scent of smoke lingering in the air. A cool breeze brushed by my face. The scent would be leaving soon enough.

The main double doors were wood and glass and led into an entry area quickly followed by a metal detector. Moline got to go around. I had to go through the thing, though my wallet, which was tucked into a pocket, set it off the first time. I had to go back through and the wallet went through on a conveyor belt alone. Then, I had to wait while they looked through the thing, examining each quarter as if it would suddenly grow spikes and become a mini shuriken.

Finally, I could follow Officer Moline past the reception desk and into a hallway lined with doors. There was no way Havestad had this many interview rooms, so some of those rooms had to be administrative offices for the department.

I'd never been in an interview room before. This one looked almost comfortable with metal folding chairs without padding and a narrow table. It didn't smell as bad as the car and the paint looked fresh. There was even a wood bench bolted down along the back wall, though I wasn't sure what that was for. On the other side were a pair of metal office chairs, again without padding.

I settled into the chair that faced the mirror on the

wall. Someone was probably watching me. I kept my face neutral.

The irony of the fact that the first time I got pulled into the police department, an interview room, not a holding cell waiting for an attorney to get me out, was when I hadn't done a damned thing.

I hadn't planned on giving up my side business, but I'd hated the drive to Duluth too much to continue doing it. The prices I could charge selling didn't make it worthwhile. I didn't even have a stash in my room anymore, not that I'd gone cold turkey. Still, my classes were suddenly interesting and I had hopes of graduating.

I guess falling to what I thought of as the fifth circle of hell kept me from wanting to visit the sixth. I had no doubt my parents would find it for me if I got kicked out again, or had too many warnings and probationary actions on my record. At the rate I was going, I wasn't even certain I could get into another private college.

I crossed my arms and waited, stomach growling. I felt myself getting rather hangry. I had little patience for this. I figured making me sit there was part of the game, to make me wait and sweat and spend time stewing in my own hunger so that I'd confess just to get a bite to eat.

Charla Moline didn't come back to the room. Officer David Andrews did. Andrews looked like he was barely out of high school. The skin of his cheeks was smoother than mine and I wondered if he even shaved. His hair was dark and silky, like a baby. His eyes were hazel under thick black eyebrows. There were women who would die for his cheekbones. While he looked like a baby now, when he reached forty or fifty, he'd be a looker.

He wore a cheap gray sports jacket over navy trousers and a pale blue button-down that did nothing for his coloring.

After getting the initial introductions finished and the comment that we were being recorded, Andrews began the questioning in earnest.

"Ms. Andresen. You're a student, a junior, a Havestad Lutheran College." Andrews voice was thick and a little slow, more southern US than Midwestern.

"Ya. Uh huh," I said in my best Fargo imitation. I'm not sure why. Maybe it was the smoothness of his voice, the lack of any hint of the Midwestern twang I'd become used to. No one around campus used "ya," much, unless they were joking. Sometimes I'd hear a "you don't say," but not terribly often.

Andrews gave me a long look, but didn't take the bait.

"You're actually a bit short of credits for a junior, meaning you'll have to finish an extra semester before you graduate. Why is that?"

Like he didn't know.

"Changed schools." True enough, but it left volumes out.

"I see that you were asked to leave your first university, though there weren't any police charges against you. In Dubuque, you were on disciplinary probation, but you choose to leave there."

Silence.

I shrugged, hoping that was enough.

"The notes here say you sold the drugs that went into food sold to the public," Andrews said. "Did you know that would happen?"

"If I sold drugs," I said, because no one had actually pinned the drug charge on me and I wasn't going to admit it, "I wouldn't ask what people were going to do with them. I'd think that students purchasing that crap, particularly on a Christian campus, would be a bit skittish if someone asked too many questions, don't you?"

I put a slight emphasis on the Christian and kept my eyes on Andrews' eyes.

"Nevertheless, you seem to have had problems during a St. Lucia Festival before. I'm wondering if there's something in your past that comes up that requires you to act out on that day?"

I rolled my eyes. "Act out how?" I asked. "Because from where I'm sitting, I thought today was the festival. I got up and started studying in my dorm. Early this morning my roommate suggested we walk around downtown and check out the crafts while getting a coffee at the Moo. We then watched the firefighters at the church for far too long. I left her with friends to go have dinner and get back to studying. Finals are next week and I'd like to keep my GPA."

"There are approximately twenty minutes between the time you got up this morning and returned to your room that your roommate can't account for," Andrews said.

They must have been questioning Jen already. I'd been pulled into Campus Security, probably to keep us apart so we didn't know the other was getting talked to. What they hadn't known was that we'd separated already.

"I was in the bathroom. Used the toilet. Sadly, I didn't know I'd need proof, or I wouldn't have flushed," I snapped. "Then, I showered. First shower of the morning takes a bit of time for the water to warm up. Maybe you can ask the school to fix that."

Andrews stared at me. Waiting.

The silence drew on. My stomach growled. I really wanted dinner and I was getting mad.

"You know what? The women's dorms are on the north side of campus. It's at least a five-minute walk to the church and back. That'd leave me, what? Ten minutes, maybe fifteen if I were jogging, to do what I needed and get back to the room. Could someone have done something in fifteen minutes?" I demanded. "What exactly am I supposed to have done in those fifteen minutes?"

"Papers were strewn around the floor and someone lit a fire. There were traces of gasoline as well."

"And I did that in fifteen minutes, because what? I had a gas can with me, just tucked up under my coat? Oh—and if you asked my roommate, did she notice that I took my coat? Because I didn't have it, so I guess I just froze my ass off or had another coat stashed so I could burn down the church because I have issues with Lucia Bride?"

Andrews said nothing. He didn't even make notes. The recording, of course.

I waited arms crossed. They had nothing on me. I wasn't going to give them anything.

"You have to see it from our perspective. You haven't been a model student and now, in the second school you've attended in as many years, the St. Lucia Festival has been disrupted. Once again, we are without Lucia Bride." Andrews waited as if that was all logical.

While it wasn't illogical, they had nothing on me. I couldn't have done it, not with the timing. I'm many things, but I'm not a runner, so I'd have had maybe ten minutes inside the church to find a basement I didn't know they had, to set this all up.

"If you know so much about me then you also know I've never been inside the church. Add that to your timeline and you'll see that my showering makes far more sense," I snapped. My stomach growled again.

"Can I go? I don't want to miss dinner at the cafeteria. I'm not rich. I suppose I would be if I were selling all those drugs, but alas, I don't."

I waited on Andrews who sighed. I paused, listening.

He probably had someone feeding him information through an earpiece. I'd seen that on television.

However, he stood up and let me leave. "I need to remind you not to leave town."

"My parents expect me home for Christmas and I'll be leaving the day after my last final next week, which means Thursday. HLC doesn't have dorms open during the holidays so unless you want to put me up in the hotel, you'll have to find me in Wisconsin," I said.

Andrews looked like he wanted to say something, but then stopped. Finally, "Leave your parents' address with the front desk."

I followed him out as quickly as possible. It was getting late and I wanted something to eat, badly.

Officer Moline drove me back to the cafeteria. She wasn't any more talkative on the way back than she had been going to the station. Not that I blamed her. I wouldn't talk much in that car either. I had no desire for the stink to crawl into my mouth. Imagine being stuck there all day.

I hurried towards the lights of the cafeteria, hoping that they hadn't run out of all the good stuff before I'd gotten there. I was really hungry.

My hair moved slightly as if someone had pushed it aside. A chill moved through my shoulders and back. I shuddered, not thinking much of it. A breeze, probably. If I'd been further away from the building, I'd have noticed that none of the trees were moving, not a single branch.

Chapter Five

I snagged some food at the cafeteria and ate alone. There were plenty of people still eating at the long tables, but none of them were folks I could just go up to and join, though I knew a few faces from classes. Conversation swirled around me along with the smells of French fries, which were on the menu that evening. I didn't hurry to finish, but it never takes that long to eat when you're alone.

I didn't mind, not really. Usually, I had people to eat with, but everyone eats by themselves now and then. A few other people sat singly, probably more than usual, a few of them looking at phones and reading, others with textbooks propped up. One woman looked like she was trying to play piano in the air and I wondered what class she was mentally preparing herself for on Monday.

We had lefsa with dinner in honor of Lucia Bride. It should have been lussekatter, the saffron-infused buns that were traditional on the day. They were shaped like a snoozing cat with two raisins for eyes. They weren't great things, but they were traditional. However, someone must have decided that the students would get more excited about lefsa than lussekatter. It seemed like the right move.

The thin, flat lefsa was rolled up neatly, clearly flavored with plenty of butter. In addition, there were small tubs of jelly that we could use to add sweetness if we desired. There are certainly sweeter treats than lefsa, but it was a nice touch, reminding me of the holidays at home, which is probably true for most of the students.

I finished the last of my lefsa and left the building, wrapping my heavy coat tightly around my body. The darkness was complete by the time I made my way through the glass doors. It's strange to me how some nights seem darker than others.

The bright lamp lights that kept the campus safe for walkers were all just as bright as usual, but somehow the night seemed darker than normal. I suppose this is the sort of thing that starts superstitions. The night would be long. St. Lucia's Day was about the longest night of the year, when monsters were supposed to roam, though St. Lucia kept them at bay.

Okay, bastardized sort of legend. There are actually several legends that all get mixed and melded together and the joy of legends is that you never know what's actually true and what's not. I huddled in my coat, loathe to leave the shelter of the bright lights from the cafeteria building.

On normal nights, the lights pooled together, leaving long rivers of golden brightness shining against the cobbled walks. Tonight, the light puddled beneath the lamps that shone down upon the cobbles, the glow eaten at by the darkness. No guiding rivers there, just lonely little ponds surrounded by dark wastelands.

I shivered, not sure why I didn't want to walk to my dorm, not alone. In fact, a part of me wanted to just stay in the cafeteria all night and go home in the morning. It seemed safer somehow, though I couldn't have said why. As I shivered, my gloved hands inside my pockets, I noticed other people hesitating at the door. One of the other girls who I recognized from around campus, gave me a half-hearted smile as she finally stepped into the night with her friend.

I decided to hurry behind them. Safety in numbers and all. I didn't have to walk with them, just close behind them. Whatever seemed to lurk out there in the darkness would believe I was part of the group, right? And if not, if I screamed, someone would turn and help me. At least I hoped so.

My footsteps sounded too loud against the cobbles. The girls ahead of me had been talking, but they quieted about halfway to the new library, which was the first building we'd pass. There was no wind. No noise at all as if the very darkness ate any sound someone made.

I huddled in my coat wishing it covered more of me. I was like a child hiding under the covers from the creature under the bed. I walked a bit faster. The girls in front of me did the same.

Passing the front doors of the library, I noticed the bright lights inside, calling me. Except they would close in another two hours and then I'd be even more alone on campus.

Normally, students were walking around, chatting even that late at night. It's not like Havestad is a dangerous place. Students, of course, are like students everywhere with schedules that included all hours of the day or night, particularly on a Saturday, even if it was the Saturday before finals. It would be the last Saturday party of the semester for those who were into that kind of thing.

The campus might be dry, but that didn't stop parties in private dorm rooms, provided they stayed just quiet enough to keep the Resident Assistant from having to check things out. Women would have to be out of the men's dorms at eleven at night and men out of the women's dorms by the same time.

Instead, tonight I walked virtually alone in the darkness but for the young women I followed. A lone young man jogged over from the north side of campus towards the library, carrying a backpack. A trickle of sweat ran down the side of his head. He didn't even look at us, but kept his eyes on the cobbles.

The emptiness was as creepy as the darkness that appeared to eat the light. I wanted to be back at my dorm, not out walking. Even in the city, I've never felt so nervous about being out after dark and I've walked in less than savory areas later than I should.

I looked over my shoulder. I thought I saw a shadow of something blacker than the darkness fade away from my sight. I whipped my head around, heart thudding.

I debated starting to run for the dorms. I could yell at the two women, but deep down I knew I wasn't going to make a sound. A sound would draw them. More of them. Whatever "them" were.

Still, I breathed harder than I should, walked as fast as I could without starting to run. The women in front of me moved quickly, too, as if aware that there was something besides a fellow student behind them.

The path between the new library and the old library building that now housed the little mathematics department was lined with trees that flowered pink in the spring and dropped their leaves the beginning of October. We'd stomped and jumped through the small piles two months ago. Now, their long skeletal limbs reached out to grab me.

Lights were placed between the trees on either side to keep this from being the perfect place to attack a student and run. I saw shadows moving from tree to tree, the slightest movement that drew my attention, only for me to miss exactly what I was looking at.

The lights from the math building lit up the path more brightly than other areas, but even there shadows lurked near the bushes at the base of the five-story brick mansion. The grilled windows looked like nothing so much as a million eyes all staring at me.

I regretted the food I ate, feeling it hovering at the base of my throat. Any little thing would make me vomit it all back up.

One of the women in front of me grabbed her friend's arm with both her hands. They kept moving quickly, but they stood closer together as if they'd seen something ahead that I'd missed while chasing shadows to the sides of us.

Beyond the math building was the cobbled quad with the four women's dorms, all four or five stories high. The nearest on the right was my ancient building, bricks blackened over time, and which had seen a million student parties in the years it had been a dorm. The newer buildings were lighter brick and wood, more evenly built with a belly full of young women in mind.

I hurried to my dorm while the two other girls hurried towards one of the more uniform buildings on the left.

I practically broke into a run, no matter that there were lit lamps along the walk and lights came from dozens of windows. The doors at each of the buildings had bright spotlights shining out along the short path to each door.

Yet I still felt alone in the darkness.

I picked up my pace until I was practically running. I felt a breath of wind at my neck. I didn't dare turn, imaging a skeletal creature about to grab me. I reached out for the door just as it was pushed open from inside. A woman starting out, stepping back when she saw me.

She didn't seem scared, not the way I felt. Still, I made it over the threshold in time to see a fleeting shadow disappear behind me.

I breathed out, feeling safe for the moment.

It wouldn't last.

Chapter Six

I studied far into the night. Jen lay across her bed, making notes. She had originally planned to go hang out with friends, but had decided against it, though only after putting on her coat and gloves and heading down-stairs to the main door. I was glad she was staying in. From the sounds of music playing in the halls and a couple of televisions, it sounded like lots of people had made the same decision.

That wasn't normal, particularly since there didn't seem to be that many visitors, and those who were visiting lived elsewhere in our dorm. A strange tension seemed to seep into the very walls that belied the logical explanation of people wanting to do well on their finals.

The smell of popcorn wafted through the dorm over-taking the spicy aroma of pizza. I heard several women in our wing complain about delays in pizza delivery. In a small town, we're spoiled. The pizza place knows it makes money delivering to students and always hires extra people for those hours when students are most likely to order. We get our pizzas hot and fast. Even the weekend before midterms the timing had been pretty accurate.

Tonight the pizzas were delivered perhaps forty minutes past the promised times, which I'd never heard of. Neither had those in the dorm with far more experience of pre-finals eating. When the woman delivering to my next-door neighbor finally got there, I couldn't help but notice her haunted eyes and the fact that she glanced around behind her back multiple times, as if worried that someone I couldn't see was behind her.

When Jen suggested a snack, while my stomach craved pepperoni and sausage, I suggested popcorn. I had no desire to force someone else out into that darkness, though I couldn't have explained what bothered me, not without sounding crazy.

It was nearly midnight when I decided to turn off my desk lamp and get ready for bed. That left only the small light Jen was reading by on over in her corner of the room. It might have been quaint and sweet but for the tension that seemed to creep around me, making the hairs on the back of my neck raise for no apparent reason. The blinds over my desk weren't yet closed and I moved to shut them. A distorted face peered back at me through the window.

I screamed. Not a scream suggesting someone was killing me with a knife and come get help, but rather a short, cut off scream that suggested I'd seen a particularly nasty bug and while surprised I wasn't really afraid.

Jen looked up. "What?" She yawned.

"There's a face at the window." I stood staring out at it. The thing out there had a long nose, crooked and bent, rather like a cartoon witch or gnome. Its skin wrinkled against a skull, a face potentially without fat to give it shape and softness, hard edges sheering away from cheekbones and chin. Thin tufts of gray and black hair stuck to the skull, but leaving part of the skull bald, not unlike Golem in *Lord of the Rings*, but not exactly like it either.

There's something almost cute about Golem. This creature was anything but cute.

The eyes were wide and narrow, long black slits in the pupils surrounded only by white. A narrow slash for a mouth, as if someone had been drawing and the pencil slipped, leaving a dark line across the face, slightly crooked.

It stared back at me. Jen got up and the image faded.

"I don't see it," she said.

Given that her pale skin had gotten lighter in the moments she'd stood near me, I didn't quite believe her.

"I did," I insisted. If there was something out there, people needed to know.

"We're on the fourth floor. No one is that tall," Jen said. "People can't fly. We'd have heard a ladder, not that I think ladders go up this high, not unless they're using a firetruck ladder or something."

She made like she was going to move closer to the window to look down, though the back of the dorm had only the utility road behind it. At the last minute, she stopped and instead shook her head and headed back to her bed. I noticed that she left the small light on even as she crawled under the covers, her book forgotten.

I did the same in my own bed. I really needed to go to the bathroom, but if something could look into the windows, it could be out in the hall. The music still playing in the dorm was faint, coming from another wing. I didn't hear anyone stirring near our room, which was particularly unprotected back in a corner, near the fire stairs.

It took a long time to fall asleep that night. Every bump and thump startled me. I heard Jen tossing and turning in her bed across the room. The music eventually went off and then there were only the sounds of the radiator creaking and groaning. I heard no one getting up to use the bathroom. The usual faint sounds of plumbing were absent.

Something scraped against the window, like a tree branch, though there were no trees close enough to reach the window. I turned my head to see what was going on. Jen pulled the blanket over her head, a child's answer to a monster. I'd have done the same but for the sense that these monsters were real and no amount of hiding under blankets would help.

Nothing appeared in the window and the sound didn't come again, though my ears strained for it.

By morning, I was dragging. I fell asleep somewhere around five, though it was still dark out. I suppose there was something about the sense that dawn was coming, a smell or faint traces of pink on the horizon that meant that the sun would soon be up that gave me comfort. Given my lack of sleep, it was going to be a hell of a day to try and study.

I slept until nine when my bladder demanded I get up. I noticed that Jen was still hidden beneath her blankets so I attempted to move as quietly as possible. A few other people stirred in the dorm. I heard a cough and the sound of a closet door closing. Someone had made coffee.

If I didn't know that the Moo would be overcrowded, I'd have gone there to get something. Instead, I'd just make do with the Keurig. It was early enough that I could grab some breakfast at the cafeteria. I couldn't imagine that the campus felt as frightening as it had last night.

On the way out, I met up with Naomi, a girl from down the hall. She's one of those tiny, petite girls that remind you of a sprite flitting from flower to flower. Her burgundy colored hair blended nicely with her fair skin.

Large brown eyes were the best feature of her heart-shaped face, though I couldn't say she had a bad feature.

Boys were always in the hall outside her door. If there was anything more unusual than the fact that everyone stayed in last night, it was that Naomi hadn't had a parade of would-be suitors quite literally knocking at her door.

Naomi was also a business major so although she was only a sophomore and I was pretty much a junior, we had some classes together. She was in the math course that I needed to retake because I hadn't passed it at PLU my last semester, nor had I managed to make it up at community college while home.

"I was just kind of out of it last night, you know?" Naomi said, chattering away, easily. "Maybe it was knowing the church had burned or something, but I didn't feel like going anywhere. I didn't even go for dinner. I had some microwave meals in the freezer and had one of those."

I nodded. The church wasn't actually part of the campus, but that was where most students were encouraged to go to worship. Campus ministers held chapel there Monday, Wednesday, and Friday. Sunday the regular church pastor held Sunday services, one early and one late. I never attended, though I had seen Naomi dressed up at breakfast sometimes on Sunday.

"It feels weird not to go to church during advent. It's one of my favorite seasons," Naomi went on. "And I loved the Lucia Bride Ceremony last year. I'd heard about it before, but I hadn't ever gone to one, you know? It's not like our city has one."

Naomi was from some smallish city in North Carolina, though I could never remember which one. There weren't a lot of Lutherans there, but they did have a Lutheran church. It was no surprise that they didn't have a ceremony. In fact, I was surprised she'd heard about it at all. For all my parents appeared devoted to their faith, I hadn't heard of Lucia Bride until I went to PLU.

I rubbed my nose in response because really I didn't have one. Naomi didn't notice, moving on to how cold it was.

"I can't believe people live here and love it. I thought I'd like snow, but I'm not sure anymore. I'll be glad when I finish and can go back to a warmer climate! No more job hunting in Minnesota for me!" Naomi laughed, her voice a low tinkle of chimes.

"You weren't in the Lucia Bride Court?" I asked. I knew that six girls had been chosen and it was just a matter of crowning the Lucia Bride.

"I was nominated," Naomi said, "But I guess my essay on my leadership capabilities wasn't good enough to get me on the court. Still, it was quite an honor. I guess two of my professors put my name in!"

I nodded. I wasn't exactly anyone's choice for the person who represents the best qualities of the student body. Of course, only sophomores were eligible. Technically, I wasn't quite a junior so I kind of could have been nominated. I'm not sure what my parents would have done if they'd heard I'd been nominated. I can't say I was certain I'd tell them should I have walked into an alternate universe where I was a role model.

Gray clouds hovered off to the north, hanging low, looking like ominous space ships about to attack. We'd have snow by evening, though I hadn't looked to see how much. I actually kind of like snow, for all I hate the cold. If there's a good part about living in the north it's the first snowfall before everything has a chance to get dirty white and scummy. Besides, the white blanket on the ground brightens the world and after last night, it seemed like we needed something to brighten the world.

Naomi and I nodded at other groups of students as we neared the cafeteria. To my eye, there seemed to be fewer of them than usual, but it was Sunday before finals so lots of folks might be sleeping in or perhaps deciding to celebrate at one of the real restaurants in town. I didn't get the sense of menace that I had last night, at least, so although I didn't see so many people, I didn't feel as if I were alone.

The cafeteria was emptier than usual. The long folding tables that sat in rows had plenty of empty chairs. Though there were only two of us, Naomi and I could have a table to ourselves if we wanted. The burnt coffee carafes were full and there was no wait for the waffle maker, though I had chosen eggs and sausages over waffles.

When Naomi and I had both scanned our phones where you paid, I said, "It seems quiet here this morning. Is Sunday before finals always this quiet?"

Naomi shook her head, leading me to the first long table. It had been freshly wiped, probably by a bored cafeteria worker.

"Never," she said. I set my tray down on the hard brown faux-wood surface and settled in one of the lightly upholstered armless chairs, arms and backs the same wood color as the table.

"Weird," I said.

"It was too quiet on campus, too. I mean, normally I'm in church, but this just feels off, you know? Like everyone is hiding in their dorms." Naomi shook her head again and dug into her eggs.

I mirrored her eating, not wanting to talk about the sense of menace I had felt yesterday. I considered telling her what had happened to me last night, but I didn't know how she'd take my tale. A few other students who had come in about the same time we did all found seats, not together, but scattered around. Four guys sat at the far end of our table, their smooth-skinned faces suggesting they were freshmen.

Naomi gave them a smile and went back to eating. I nodded in their direction, but said nothing. I had a feeling that they considered themselves brave sitting this close to Naomi.

The guys weren't talking quietly. "Much better than last night," the dark-haired guy in a red jacket said. Only four seats separated us so his voice was clear.

"Creeped me out last night," the guy next to him said, his long blonde hair hitting the sides of his face as he shook his head. I think his hair was longer than mine.

"I ran for the dorm!" the black-haired guy on Naomi's side replied.

"I practically shit," said Red Jacket. "I mean I felt something touch the back of my neck. Like something not human."

"Woo ooohhh ohhhh" the last guy made a face as he sang a ghostly theme.

"You weren't there. Ordered pizza in. You might want to consider why you did that," Longhair snapped. He didn't look pleased.

Their conversation moved on to how it was good that the pizza delivery folks weren't afraid of the dark and could get them food.

On the one hand, I liked that the sense that there was something out there didn't mean I was going crazy, but on the other hand, I hated that there might actually be something out there.

As Naomi and I were finishing our breakfast, quietly making a bit of small talk about our upcoming vacations,

Red Jacket turned the conversation back to the night before.

"You don't suppose that burning down the church let out ghosts or something? You know, they can't rest because the church is gone?"

"You watch too many horror movies, idiot," the unbeliever said. He sounded annoyed that the conversation had gone back to the night before. I wondered if the annoyance came because he had sensed something, but was no more eager to admit it than I was.

Maybe we did all watch too many horror movies, but that didn't mean there might not be something to the idea that the church burning down started this. Maybe it had let something out, something only a church could keep contained. I felt stupid even thinking it. A movie cliché if there ever was one.

Still, it wasn't a thought I wanted to pursue more closely, nor did I want to hear more ideas about what had happened last night. I might have to accept the fact that the freshmen guys and I weren't just giving into our imaginations on a particularly dark and quiet night.

Thankfully, Naomi and I picked up our trays about that time so we could head back to the dorm. We both had some studying to do.

We were in the quad in front of the four women's dorms when someone started screaming from between the two dorm buildings across the way from ours, one of which was the dorm the two women who'd walked in front of me the night before had entered.

Naomi and I looked at each other before heading over there to see what was going on.

Chapter Seven

I dreaded what I might see. I pictured the women in front of me last night, though all I could remember of them was their brown hair and heavy jackets. They'd been ordinary campus women, neither fat nor thin and I hadn't known either one except to see them around. If one of them were injured and had lain outside all night, they couldn't have survived.

Stepping closer, I noticed the navy blue coat and heavy boots for walking. Then I saw the orange vest our pizza delivery drivers always wore. The haunted, worried look on the face of the woman delivering to our dorm flashed into my mind. The slow delivery times.

Other pizza delivery drivers might be lying on the ground between dorms and I tamped down a need to go searching between buildings for someone else. Not just because I didn't want to find a body and the questions that would come out about why I decided to look for more people, but because I didn't need to feed my worries. Acting on them felt as if it would make them real. Or maybe more real.

I belatedly pulled out my phone, but before dialing 911, I noticed other students doing the same. No need to tie up the lines. I backed up. Naomi stood where she was, shaking. A couple of other women were kneeling beside the body, one calling out orders that were only beginning to register in my mind.

I touched Naomi's arm. She didn't even glance over at me. Her gaze was riveted on the body lying on the frozen ground.

The gray clouds above us started to send flurries of tiny snowflakes down around our heads. Because the morning wasn't bad enough.

"Naomi?" I said. I didn't yell. Didn't whisper. Spoke in a normal tone of voice because that was most likely to draw her attention. Nothing from Naomi, but a couple of other people looked my way.

"Naomi?" I said again, a bit louder, a hand on her shoulder, pulling her back.

Finally, she looked over at me. "What?" she asked.

"You're shivering," I said. "We should go inside." Chances were she wouldn't warm up inside. I understood the cold she was feeling and felt the internal chill creeping up my spine. I wanted nothing so much as to flee from Havestad and hide in my bed at home for the rest of my life. I didn't have that choice though. I had to finish school and at least had to finish the semester at HLC.

Naomi nodded and let me lead her to our dorm across the way. She said nothing and if I didn't have a hand on her, she stopped moving. It was as if only my touch let her know what to do next. She was in shock and I worried that by taking her away from the scene I was taking her away from potential help. If she needed it, we could call someone later. For now, a familiar place and a heavy blanket, perhaps some hot cocoa, which I kept in my room, would help.

I talked soothingly to her the entire way back. A few students came out and were looking at the growing crowd between the other two dorms. Everyone wanted to know what was going on. I had a feeling more than a few had felt the creepiness of the campus last night.

The dorm was noisier than usual on a Sunday morning. Gone was the emptiness of earlier. Death brought everyone out of their holes.

Gossip swirled around. I heard that a pizza delivery person was murdered by a serial killer, a ghost, had dropped a truck load of pizzas in the yard, was found having sex with the Dean of Admissions, and had been knocked over the head by someone stealing their pizzas.

I watched more than one girl go out with jeans and a heavy coat over a pajama top, checking on what was happening. On our floor, the room midway down on the side overlooking the cobbled quad, had the door open and half a dozen women were pressed against the glass at the far side of the room, watching.

Fortunately, Naomi's room faced the other direction and I opened her door and escorted her in. Her roommate wasn't around. I helped Naomi take off her coat and her boots and wrapped her blankets around her after she was settled on her bed. Hopefully, she'd snap out of it.

I headed further down the hall to my room. Jen was there, sitting on the loveseat staring at the refrigerator.

"What's up?" I asked. No book sat in Jen's lap. She was still in her pajamas. She didn't have any coffee or tea with her.

"My mom called," Jen said.

I noted the cell phone lying next to her leg where it had likely fallen to the side when she'd finished the call.

"Is everything okay at home?" I asked. She acted as if someone had died.

"My mom is superstitious," Jen said. "She's worried that the last couple of years several Lucia Bride Ceremonies have been canceled and she thinks that bad things will happen after dark. And just as she warned me to go out and get some groceries for the week so I didn't have to eat dinner in the cafeteria, I heard about the pizza delivery person."

I felt a light sweat break out along my forehead. My hands felt cold and clammy. I pulled off my gloves, hoping the air in the room would help them dry and warm them, at least a little bit. My core felt chilled and I needed to huddle beneath a blanket.

"That's probably a coincidence?" I hated the way my voice went up at the end, a question, not a statement.

"Except you don't believe that do you?" Jen said, looking at me. "You were weird when you came back from dinner. I know the police questioned you. They questioned me about your whereabouts yesterday morning. We didn't do anything, but they wanted to know stuff. You didn't even mention it when you came in."

"Did you go to dinner?" I asked.

Jen nodded. "It was kind of creepy coming back to the dorm, but there was a bunch of us. I figured it was just stress, even though this is my third year and I don't generally stress about finals, not so badly I think I see shadows moving. But then again, I haven't just watched a church burn either."

"Me either," I said. "I had a bit of trouble at my other school. You probably figured that out."

"You've said. You never mentioned what it was."

"I could get things. Drugs," I told her. "And I sold some to the wrong people. I guess some of the NorthStar

Dancers at St. Lucy's were making very special St. Lucia buns and they were selling them to the public. The school found out I had been selling. I never admitted it, so they couldn't prove it and kick me out, but I got put on disciplinary probation. My folks were pissed and decided that Dubuque was a bad influence on me and made me switch schools."

Jen smiled a little and nodded. "I think my mom heard that Lucia Bride was canceled last year because of the weird lussekatter." Jen would, of course, know the correct name of the buns.

"But Lucia Bride went on here?" I pressed.

"Normal as always," Jen said. "I was part of the court, though I wasn't Lucia Bride."

"Why is your mom worried about Lucia Bride not happening?" That didn't make sense. I mean, her worries made sense, but her reasoning was lost on me. As I started thinking more clearly, opening my jacket to hang it up, I realized I didn't understand.

"Between St. Lucia's Day and Yule are the darkest nights of the year, or so the legend goes. During that time, trolls and other dark creatures and evil ghosts roam during the nights causing mischief. Those are all based on legends of someone called Lussi who might or might not be Lilith by another name. At any rate, in my mom's family there's this belief that only St. Lucy and her light keep the creatures at bay," Jen said. "So here I am without a Lucia Bride to keep the light going and my mom is certain that horrible things will happen."

"And then you heard about the pizza delivery person. She was here, you know. Last night, late. She looked kind of scared about being out and about. Which creeps me out. She could have been afraid of someone she knew, too, though. A human."

Jen nodded. "Probably. But after you saw the face…"

"You didn't. I could have been half asleep…"

"I saw it." Jen held my eyes. "I just couldn't believe it. Not then. But after my mom…Could she be right?"

The idea of Lucia Bride holding off the things that go bump in the night was not a legend I'd ever heard of. I hadn't researched it a whole lot, but the first year I'd heard about the festival at PLU I had looked it up on the internet. I thought it was a made-up holiday to show off their Mayfest Dancers. I was wrong. It really was a holiday and celebrated in the United States and Scandinavia and maybe even Italy.

I remembered reading a little about Lussi, but hadn't heard the connection with Lilith, though I wasn't sure who that was and didn't really care to find out. The way things were going, she'd be some dark badass goddess with a hate-on for pizza delivery drivers.

Maybe that was why I hadn't been that surprised that Jen's mom had brought up St. Lucia Day and the festival. Maybe in the back of my mind, I understood things I didn't think I knew.

"It was creepy walking back from the cafeteria," I said. "I thought I saw something following me or alongside the walk. I couldn't really see it though. Just shadows."

Jen nodded. "No one wanted to go out, either."

"And we can't ask other people to deliver our meals if the delivery people are being hurt, too. We ought to go grocery shopping," I said. I didn't have the funds, not really, but I'd text my mom and let her know I needed to use the debit card. She was on my account. She'd see it was for the little grocery store in town. I'd just say I wanted to have extra food for studying and text her a copy of the receipt. It would make her happy to think of me studying.

Perhaps it's wrong to lie to my mom about stuff like

that, but if I tried to explain to her about trolls and creatures of the night, she'd be certain I was using again and I'd end up somewhere worse. I planned to graduate from HLC so I'd have to make do with a little white lie. Hopefully, my grades would hold up well enough to make her believe I had at least tried to study.

Chapter Eight

J en and I went shopping. It meant we missed the body being taken away from between the buildings. Lots of students stood watching, despite the fact that snow began to fall harder. By the time we returned with plenty more popcorn, which would last forever, easy mix soups, some microwavable burritos that we could tuck into our small freezer, and even some cold chicken that we could grab for that evening, the snow was falling harder still. No longer a few flurries or even a light shower, this was a storm.

Tiny flakes blasted at our faces. The low gray clouds hovered barely above my head and fog lingered around trees making the entire campus feel haunted. With a recent death near our dorm, it might have felt haunted on the sunniest of days. The dark clouds and weather made the sensation worse.

Shadows moved from tree to tree while we walked quickly through the paths that led us back to the dorm. We'd walked to the store because it was only a few blocks and would take nearly as long to unload a car if we had driven there.

When our voices seemed to echo into the odd surroundings, Jen and I both quieted and just walked as quickly as we could through the snow. Not many people were out any longer. Near the dorm, yellow crime scene tape made a stark contrast to the grays of the day and the white snow that now dusted the grass.

Police officers were still there, bright spotlights shining on the crime scene which had been placed beneath a tent. The place where the body had lain remained free of snow, but not completely without fog, despite the lights and the covering. I didn't envy the officers working, one of which looked like Officer Moline, who had escorted me so silently to the police station the night before. Other officers weren't in uniforms and I wondered if Havestad had its own detective unit or if they had to call in the county sheriffs.

I was chilled through when Jen and I got back inside. The warmth hit me through all my layers and I quickly threw back the hood of my jacket and let my hair swing free. Small drops of water hit the ground around me.

"Nasty day to go shopping," Patti, who was on front desk duty, said quietly. Her red hair had been woven into a neat French braid and she sat eating soup brought over from the cafeteria.

"Nasty day to have someone go out and get food from the cafeteria," Jen said. "I'm not sure I'd have done it for you." All with a smile and a laugh which elicited another laugh from Patti. Jen was easy with people in a way I am not. I'd have sounded snarky serious if I'd tried that and Patti would have been pissed off at me for weeks, if not months.

Among other duties, when we got snail mail, the front desk people sort it into our little mailboxes. They also kept our packages and let us know when they were there. I might not get many letters, but I did get packages now and again. If I pissed Patti off, she might not let me know I had a package. If I didn't pick it up within three days, it would be returned. I mean, I didn't know that. No one had complained about Patti, but there had been rumors about one front desk person at St. Lucy's.

"It's horrible about the pizza woman," Jen went on, pausing to chat. I waited before going up, hanging back, listening a little.

"Isn't it? Officers even came in here wanting to talk to people whose windows overlooked the quad. I had to call the Dorm Mom to have her clear it. The RAs all had to listen in on the interviews, just in case," Patti said.

I understood the excitement in her voice, that sense of being a part of something important and different, something that would be talked about for months, if not years.

"And can you imagine? First, the church burns down and now someone's been murdered," Patti said. "What a horrible holiday season for the people of Havestad!"

Clearly, Patti was a better person than I was. I hadn't even thought about how this would affect the locals. All I'd thought about was how it affected me and by extension, other students. At least I'd considered that if I were in danger, a pizza delivery person would be in danger, too.

I'd be leaving on Friday morning to head home. The locals had to stay. I should ask Jen how long we had to be worried and how far the effect went. I mean did Lucia Bride just protect this town or did she hold a larger area of influence?

Patti and Jen gossiped a bit, but I learned nothing new. One other pizza delivery person hadn't shown up to work last night so they'd been behind. Now they were short two people with one found dead and the other still missing.

"I hope there's not some deranged serial killer killing pizza delivery drivers," Patti said in a hushed voice, looking around to make sure no one overheard. She needn't have worried. We were alone in the front reception area, all the other dorm dwellers hanging out in their rooms or their friends' rooms probably talking about the murder.

Jen and I headed up the stairs. I was pleased to hear plenty of voices coming from the various floors of the dorm. I even heard the squeal of the elevator going down. It would probably take whoever was in the elevator longer to reach the ground floor than it would take Jen and me to reach our floor going up. The thing was nearly as old as the building and I had no trust that it wasn't going to hang between floors someday.

On our floor, Naomi was wrapped in a blanket. I noted that she'd changed into sweats while I'd been gone. "Thanks for making sure I got back here," Naomi said as I went past. "I was really freaked out. I've never seen a dead person before…except in movies, you know?"

I nodded. "I'm glad you seem better."

Naomi nodded, her eyes down. Better might not have been the best choice of words. She was still upset, but at least she wasn't in shock any longer.

Reaching our room, putting away our haul I asked Jen, "Did your mom say how long this would last? The night stuff?"

Jen shook her head. "I think it's through Yule, but I'm not sure. After that, the nights get shorter again and aren't considered as dark."

"Is it everywhere or just Havestad?"

"I don't know. I mean every place that has a Lucia Bride Ceremony contributes to the light. Some years they get missed. I think this area is most affected and probably further south because of the fiasco in Dubuque last year. I mean, it couldn't be everywhere could it?"

As I put away a pint of ice cream, squeezing it into the freezer, I wondered if someone had set the church on fire on purpose, to somehow let out the monsters of the darkest nights of the year. After all, as had been pointed out to me, the timing was interesting.

Chapter Nine

It's hard to study when you keep looking out the window, worried about seeing monsters roaming the campus instead of students. Bright spotlights from the front of the building lit even the back of the dorm where our window faced. Dark trees waved in a slight breeze, their branches but shadows in the gray day.

Jen and I heated up the cold chicken and paired it with some potato salad we had purchased at the store. We'd each purchased a bit of the chicken so there weren't arguments about who got what. We each had a couple of dishes for serving food and we used those, eating together in the dorm room, the spotlights and perhaps flashlights of people searching for another missing person flashed and moved outside.

I turned down the interior lights except for the small light over in Jen's sleeping corner and peered out to see what the moving lights were. The lights on tall poles throughout the campus kept things from being too dark, but even from here I noted how their gold color was eaten away by the darkness as if by a living thing. There were three lamps along the walk behind the dorm. No students moved back there, but the lights dimmed and brightened when the trees covered them as their branches swished in the wind.

I thought I saw a shadow out in the trees, but I couldn't imagine what anyone would be doing out there. Shadow monsters could be put down to my imagination, but the cold couldn't, and wandering in the trees so late at night, it would be easy to get turned around. It might be hard to get lost this close to town, but our dorm sat on the edge of campus so it wouldn't be impossible. Particularly not on such a dark and foggy night.

I moved away and turned on our lights while Jen and I talked and finished our dinners.

"I didn't get much done today," I said. "I'm going to miss my A in business law."

Jen nodded. "I could hardly think. I kept worrying about what happens tonight. My mom said we should be safe inside, but are we? I mean it gets dark indoors, too. It's not like we're in a house where we know no one is opening the door. People go in and out of the front at all hours."

I had read up on the hauntings by the creature called Lussi, a witch according to the articles I found. Supposedly, people were safe indoors, but no one had explained why. The walls were supposed to keep her out, but nothing had discussed whether she could walk through an open door. Vampires couldn't, not unless they'd been invited, but they were the only creatures who required an invitation that I knew of. Witches didn't.

Too bad my finals wouldn't be about the supernatural. That's what I'd spent my time reading when I should have been hitting the books on economics and business law. Considering how much I'd read, I'd probably ace about anything a professor would throw at me.

"I don't know. I mean we can keep this door closed all the time," I said.

"Bathroom," Jen responded.

It might be possible to do without showers, though it would feel icky. It was less possible to do without a toilet.

"Do you have a flashlight?" I asked. The halls were always lit, but after eleven they were only lit with emergency lights which came on when the main lights went out. They were dimmer than the main lights. The wood paneling might be stained a pale gold, but the dark seemed to eat the dull yellow light the emergency bulbs gave off. The hallway always filled with shadows that moved and swirled and probably gave rise to the rumors our dorm was haunted.

"Just on my phone," Jen said.

"We should use that when we go out." If we stayed up late, chances were other women in the dorm would still be up, too. We'd use the phone flashlight which along with the dimly lit hallway should make things bright enough. At least I hoped so.

I glanced at my Diet Coke. Maybe I shouldn't drink so much just before bed. I wouldn't have to go down the hall quite so often. I decided against a second one.

At least once I got to the bathroom, even if the room was dark, the light switch was just inside the door. The powerful lights lit the room up no matter what time of night it was. In fact, maybe we ought to prop that door open so that light from the bathroom would flood the hallway.

I asked Jen.

"I don't know. I'm not sure if everyone is as spooked as we are," she said slowly.

I thought about how quiet breakfast had been and the guys at the end of the table at breakfast. People were spooked. Someone had died in the night and they were spooked about that, too.

I got up to go wash my plate in the kitchen next door.

One of the reasons our room is so oddly shaped is that the kitchen is tucked up next to it on one side and the stairs on the other. There are no windows in the kitchen, but the lights are bright fluorescents I normally complain about. They make a buzzing noise I hate and the plastic covers over them are ugly and old enough to be turning slightly gray leaving the room with an odd cast.

But there's a bigger refrigerator, which everyone tries to avoid using lest someone steal their food, an oven that gets used mostly for baking cookies for a boyfriend, and a sink which does get used to wash dishes when people heat the food from their own little refrigerators in their own microwaves. There is a microwave in the kitchen as well, but I'm not sure it's used beyond the first week of school. After that everyone figures out it's so much easier to have one in their room.

It didn't take much time to wash our plates and forks. Glancing down the hallway, I noticed that not many room doors were open. Usually light spilled out from one or two and several people would be laughing. Katie, a freshman who lived at the far end of the hall hurried out of the bathroom, giving us only a quick glance before practically running for her room.

I followed Jen into our room and closed the door, checking to be sure it was locked. I'd have felt better if we could push a dresser in front of it, but our wardrobes and dressers were affixed to the wall and couldn't be moved.

"Okay, it's already creepy," I said. The hallway had still been brightly lit and yet everyone was already hiding in their rooms, which was exactly what I wanted to do.

Jen closed the blinds over our desks. Normally, I'd have

closed the blinds over my desk when I was ready to do so, but she wasn't taking any chances. They were old metal things that let in light at the edges of the window and in a few places where the metal had been bent at one time or another, probably because students from years past had set something on the sill and forgotten and tried to close the blinds. Overeager fingers looking out at a potential boyfriend probably bent some of the slats, too.

I didn't say a thing. Looking outside was not high on my list. I remembered the face in the window before going to bed last night. We were up high enough that we didn't always close the blinds, even when changing clothes. Not many people wandered out in the woods. I thought about the shadow I had noticed out there. Had it been a person or a tree, a trick of the light and my overstressed imagination letting me see a human-like figure where there was none?

Both of us went to our desks and settled in to pretend to study. Jen had her laptop out and was working on it. I didn't know if she was actually studying some notes she had on there or if she was playing online. I pulled out my business law book to attempt to go over some of the information I suspected would be on the final.

As interesting as that subject had always been to me, I couldn't make myself focus. I had a hard time caring about mundane laws when there were monsters on the loose.

Though it went slowly, I plowed through my reading and closed up my books at about eleven. I grabbed my phone and turned on the flashlight app I had downloaded and scurried down the hallway. I had just missed the lights being turned off and the emergency lights coming up.

I heard low music from one other room. Light seeped from beneath firmly closed doors. All of that gave me hope, though I was certain shadows moved wrongly at the far end of the hallway. I fled to the bathroom, thankful that someone had left the lights on in there.

I brushed my teeth quickly, listening to the sounds of the radiator. Someone flushed upstairs. The sound of a toilet flushing had never been so comforting. At least I wasn't alone moving around in the dorm.

I used the toilet myself. No one came or went while I was in there. Eleven isn't that late for a dorm, not the Sunday before finals. It was hard to believe that no one else had any reason to use the bathroom, not to shower, not to brush their teeth, not to pee.

I put my toiletries in the little cubby assigned to me. The cubbies were across from the sinks. Anyone with something of value kept it in their room, but the cubbies allowed us to keep toothbrushes and such in the bathroom.

I made sure my phone flashlight was on before exiting. I smelled coffee and something spicy. Someone was planning on making a late night of it.

I glanced back towards the far end of the hall, where I'd seen the shadows. The dark seemed to move, but I couldn't make anything out. For a split second I considered checking out what it was, but decided that if I were in a horror movie, that'd make me the second person killed. Instead, I hurried down the hallway as quickly as possible, looking back over my shoulder only twice.

The second time, Naomi's roommate hurried out of their room, also with a flashlight app, and practically ran to the bathroom. She looked a bit embarrassed that someone had noted her fleeing. I quickly slipped into my room and locked the door.

"You survived," Jen said. I wasn't sure if there was sarcasm there or not.

"So far," I said. I pulled on my sweats and prepared to try and sleep. I left the light on nearest the door. If anything tried to get into our room, it would have to go through the lights. I hoped it was enough.

Jen said nothing to my comment, though she looked nervously around the room as if searching the corners for anything. I crawled into bed, but not before checking beneath it. My suitcases lay on their sides tucked up underneath the mattresses. No glowing eyes peered out at me. It didn't slow my heart rate.

The sheets were cool and the covers warm, just the way I love it. However, sleep didn't come. I closed my eyes multiple times, only to allow my imagination to run wild, seeing short, shadow creatures with white teeth and red glowing eyes slipping furtively across the room near the walls.

Each time, I'd open my eyes to make sure nothing was staring at me from the foot of the bed.

Jen remained quiet. I listened for her breathing, but she sat in her bed and read, or pretended to read a textbook. I wished she'd turn in and fall asleep so that her light snores would calm my anxiety and I, too, could fall asleep. Knowing she was awake should've let me sleep, but the silence bothered me.

From outside, far away, I thought I heard a scream. Or maybe a snarl. The building shook lightly as if a large truck went by. No large trucks traversed the roads closest to the dorms and I'd never felt such a thing before.

I sat up, looking around.

Jen had heard what I heard. She sat on the bed, staring straight ahead, shoulders tense and hunched against another scream. Together, we waited.

Chapter Ten

I heard no other screams. I got up slowly and went to my desk. I squeezed into the narrow area between the desk and the wall and moved the metal slats of the blinds enough to peer out. I saw only the dim lights. No moving shadows in the trees. I couldn't imagine hearing a scream that came from the front, so it had to come from the side of the dorm or behind us.

"I don't see anything," I told Jen.

Just as I was dropping the blind, something dropped in front of my view, like a giant spider on a cord, a dark creature hanging and swinging.

Its full head of hair stuck out in all directions like a bad movie director's image of what a giant spider's head should look like. This creature only had two arms and two legs, which were far too short. It rode on a vine, which hung down from the roof. It waved at me, sharp teeth too white in its shadowed face. Its eyes were forest green and held a dark glow that surrounded its head.

I cut off a shriek before it started and dropped the blinds stepping back.

"Was it the face again?" Jen asked.

"Different one," I said. "This was a smaller creature, about the size of a toddler, but it had sharp white teeth. It waved at me. It *saw* me."

Sweat gathered around the back of my neck. I felt too hot and too cold all at once. My stomach turned and I felt the chicken from earlier attempting to rush up and out to splatter all over the floor. I clenched my teeth, holding my lips together until the illness passed.

The door to the backstairs, the ones that my bed sat next to, opened and closed. It always held a hollow sound, but tonight it felt particularly ominous. I shuddered, the heat of my flush giving way to a chill that ate through my bones.

I needed to scream, but clamped down on the impulse, not wanting to give away my position any more than I already had. I tried to breathe through the fear that made every muscle in my body clench, but my lungs found it difficult to take in any but the most minimal of air.

I heard someone running along the hallway, pounding against the wood with their boots, making the mugs that sat on the dresser shake and clank against each other. No one I knew ran through the halls like that. Tonight, though, I could imagine running for my life to get to my room.

I also imagined the creature making its way into the dorm and running amok down the hallways, waiting to catch someone opening a door to see who might be there. I wished, suddenly that we had peepholes or door cameras to tell us who might be out there. A surveillance state might be safer if those creatures really existed. I could look out and see if it was safe to leave the room.

A door slammed. Someone had probably just been scared and had run down the hall. I shuddered and moved back to my bed, my legs suddenly weak. I had to pee, though I'd gone not long ago. However, no matter what my bladder said, there was no way I was going out into that hallway.

"I'm scared," Jen said in a small voice.

"Me too." There wasn't much to say to that. I swallowed a few times, hoping to get the sense of being about to vomit out of my body.

Something pinged against the glass of our window. Jen and I didn't move. Didn't check to see if someone was throwing something at the window. We just looked at each other. Jen shrunk back in her sleeping cubby, so far into the corner I couldn't make out her face.

"Maybe we'd be safer together," I said. "I can bring my stuff and sleep on the floor over there."

The wood was hard and unforgiving. We had a rug in the center area, but it would take time to move it near Jen's bed. Plus, it wasn't very thick. I wouldn't sleep well, but at least I wouldn't be alone.

"We can pull your mattress over," Jen said. "It should fit, don't you think?"

And so we did, pulling the mattress off the low framed bed. The frame was made of wood so that the college didn't have to purchase a box spring as well. Twin mattresses weren't that heavy to flip off the bed and it was easy enough to drag it into Jen's cubby. It lay down, just barely, in the walkway between her bed and the wall. I cuddled down on it, feeling better knowing there was someone close to me.

"How can this be happening?" Jen whispered.

"Maybe call your mom in the morning and ask what else she might know. Like could they get into the dorm if someone had the front door open? Can they climb stairs?

And how the heck are we seeing faces outside our window?"

Jen nodded. She climbed over me and out of the cubby to grab her phone. She dialed her mom. It was probably after midnight.

It didn't take long for her mom to answer.

I listened to Jen's side of the conversation. I heard the things Jen told her mom. She asked our questions. Lots of I don't knows. Then I can'ts. An argument about something Jen's mom wanted her to do, but Jen didn't want to. Then something about the hotel in town.

Finally, she hung up the phone. "Mom wants me back home. She doesn't care about finals."

"But…" I stammered. Jen wouldn't want to do that. I had heard her side of the conversation.

"She's coming up tomorrow and checking into the hotel. I'm supposed to stay with her and she'll drive me to my finals. It's a compromise," Jen said. She looked at me, sort of apologetic.

"It leaves you alone here, though." Jen finished after a moment, in case I didn't get the implication.

I nodded. I gulped, but there wasn't much I could say. I didn't know Jen well enough to invite myself along to the hotel with her mom. Her mom didn't seem to particularly like me, distrusting the fact that I'd transferred from St. Lucy's before going to HLC. She wasn't going to just take me with them, much as I wished she might.

"You should see if your folks will let you stay there. You only have one late class…" Jen said.

That class was tomorrow. My economics final started at four, but it would be getting dark about that time. I wasn't sure how long the final was, but the time frame said the final lasted until six. At my other universities, that was just class time and finals rarely took the entire two hours. Even so, I'd be walking as it got dark.

The walk to the hotel was darker than the walk to the dorm, at least tomorrow. There was no way I'd be sleeping there, not tomorrow, though the idea of staying in the hotel drew me.

"I'll talk to my parents tomorrow. Tell them something is going on around the dorms," I said. "Maybe…"

I heard myself telling my parents about my fear. They'd think I'd been taking more drugs, harder drugs, things I'd never been interested in touching. They'd refuse assistance, believing it was all my imagination, no matter that my roommate had left for the hotel. They might even believe she was using, too, though my mother had seemed to approve of Jen when they'd met.

My stomach twisted and turned, not trying to vomit any longer but merely to knot itself up in hopes of wringing the fear out of me. I breathed in and laid down on the mattress in the cubby.

Jen would probably help me move my mattress back in the morning. Or not. I wasn't sure it mattered. In some ways, sleeping on the floor near her bed felt safer than in my own cubby. I didn't know why.

After a long while, I heard her breathing become more even and light. She'd fallen asleep. I lay there, trying to keep tears from falling, wondering if I was going to die tomorrow night. And if I didn't die, what sorts of terrors would I face?

Chapter Eleven

Jen packed up her stuff for the holidays and was gone before I even left for my final. She wouldn't go home until Thursday but she'd be safer in the hotel with her mom. At least there they had a door with a heavier lock and they wouldn't have to go down a hall for a bathroom.

"I hate leaving you," Jen said. "I asked Mom about it, really. But there are only two beds in the room and she wants some space." Jen shook her head as if her mom was being ridiculous and this reaction was unexpected.

It wasn't unexpected to me.

At least Jen left a lot of her soups and stuff in the room. "I guess you'll have plenty of food for the evening," she said. "Lots of choices."

She ended up hugging me goodbye. We're roommates, but not close, not like a lot of women are with the people they room with in college. We didn't normally hug. We didn't often hang out, other than for meals when neither of us, or rather Jen, had no one better to eat with. I'd say companionable more than friends. Suddenly, Jen was my friend, or wanted to believe she was.

Cynical me figured she'd feel better about herself if something happened to me and she'd acted like a friend and not just someone sharing space. It made no difference to me in the long run. If I were going to be in danger, I'd be in danger whether she was friendly or not.

Alone in the room, I did get studying done until I had to leave for my final. The shadows were already gathering towards dusk. Sunset was something like 4:20 PM, give or take depending upon how accurate a watch was, but though the snow had stopped, clouds remained low over the town. Light fog drifted around the corners of buildings. The cold made my steps hurry towards the business building which was halfway across campus.

The building was one of the newer ones just past the cafeteria. The lights were all on along the walks. The campus buildings all appeared to be lit up as much as possible, though the gray clouds and gathering fog gobbled as much light as the darkness had the other night. I dreaded walking back to the dorm.

Beyond the cafeteria, the business building rose, shiny steel and glass. Lights shone from the windows of each of the classrooms and from the windows of the large confer- ence center downstairs. I'd never seen the place so bright. The department offices had strung Christmas lights and those were on, which was to be expected, but every single faculty office had light glowing from their window. That wasn't expected.

I hurried in. A few students were in the lobby, looking out at the failing light.

One girl was breathing in deeply as if about to dive down into the ocean or perhaps planning to make a long sprint. A blonde guy was slowly buttoning a jacket, trying not to look worried. He kept glancing at the others, perhaps hoping someone would walk with him across the darkening campus. I envied his debate, the fact that he got to have it now and not in two hours or however long it took me for my final.

The door opened behind me. A tall, red-haired girl named Lisa walked through. She was in my class. She lived off campus because her family lived in town. I didn't envy her the walk to the parking lot. The parking area for students who lived off-campus was further from the building than my dorm. I didn't see a flashlight, though I saw anxiety in her face.

"Hey," I said. I might have just walked alone across campus and hated it, but I'd take any known face, even inside. The creatures weren't supposed to get inside, but Jen's mom hadn't had a good answer and so far she was my only source about what was going on.

"Hey," Lisa said. Her hair hung over her heavy black coat in a single braid. It fell at least to the edges of her shoulder blades. Her fair skin looked paler than normal. I thought I saw freckles dotting her nose, something I'd never noticed before.

"You ready?" I asked, making conversation.

"I'm terrified," Lisa said.

I didn't know how to respond to that. Was she terrified of what was going on outside in town or was she terrified of the economics final? I swallowed, trying to decide how to proceed.

"Not about the final, exactly, but about this timing. If my parents hadn't insisted, I'd have skipped out. It's going to be full dark before we get out and I'll have to walk all the way across campus. Someone died here the last two nights," Lisa said.

I was surprised I hadn't heard about someone last night. "I knew about the pizza driver..." I started.

"An old man out getting his mail died last night. He

lives at the edge of town and his driveway is probably half a mile from his house, all under trees. They found him late yesterday. I doubt it made news on campus, but my uncle doesn't live far from him. My mother is freaking out."

"Wow," I said. There was nothing more to say as we walked down the shiny white tile halls, all brightly lit with bulbs that seemed to be higher wattage than usual. Or maybe it was just that I wasn't used to light coming out of every single open door, though given the quietness of the hallways, there weren't that many students around.

Two freshmen guys walked past us, hurrying along to their final. They turned at the next open doorway on my left. One of the largest classrooms in the building, taking up three times the size of the one Lisa and I had class in.

We continued past the door. I glanced at the bulletin board that hung on the cream wall just outside the room. A few notices for people needing to rideshare to get home. A couple to the airport in Duluth. I'd read them all last week as they'd started getting hung on the wall.

"When's your last final?" Lisa asked.

"Thursday morning," I said. I would have left for home Thursday afternoon, but wasn't sure I wanted to chance driving after dark. My morning final was at ten. Assuming I got out early, I still wouldn't be leaving before noon by the time I loaded my car. At that point, it would take until after dark to get home.

Lisa nodded. "I'd recommend not going home until Friday. Stay at the hotel and treat yourself or something. Better still, treat yourself to a nice place in Duluth."

"Like I have that kind of money," I said. I kept a smile on my face.

Lisa said nothing for a moment. As we reached the door and slipped inside the classroom, she spoke. "Murders don't happen here in Havestad. And from what my folks have heard, the police chief is perplexed as to how they died. The pizza delivery driver was just dead. My uncle's neighbor looked like he'd been half-eaten but the teeth marks don't match a bear."

I tried to suppress a shudder. "Scary," I whispered. The quiet room had me wanting to step softly and not draw attention to myself. Lisa headed to her usual seat and I slipped in beside Chris who was already there, a book open on his desk.

"Ready?" I asked, still keeping my voice quiet.

"I slept for shit last night," he mumbled. "And I had a final this morning, too. So no. Not really. And economics doesn't interest me the way law does. I could hardly concentrate especially because we had a guy sure something had chased him to the dorm and he was still screaming when he got there, probably well after midnight. They ended up taking him to the hospital."

"I think we might have heard some of that even in the girls' dorms," I said.

Chris nodded. "Kept us all up half the night. I guess locals who know the legends say that because there wasn't a Lucia Bride this year the creatures of the night are coming out to play. Supposed to last until Yule. I can't believe I looked up to see the last time there wasn't a Lucia Bride crowned here."

"When was it?" I asked, trying to smile, but I was hanging on his words, eager to look up the information myself or at least what happened that year.

"It hasn't happened here before," Chris said. "It's not a big festival but there's always been someone crowned by the thirteenth of December to have her court until the next bride is crowned."

"It happened in Dubuque last year," I said. "I don't

think anything happened." I wasn't ready to add that Jen's mom thought that was part of the problem.

Chris nodded. "A guy in my dorm is certain that's part of the problem. I can't believe people here are that superstitious. I was willing to go to a Lutheran school because they said religion and crap wasn't required and yet I'm being kept awake because folks are terrified of ghouls and ghosts."

"I hear trolls are big during this time, too," I said.

Chris gave me a look.

I shrugged. "You did your research. I did mine. Remember, our dorm was near where the pizza delivery woman was killed."

"Like that helps all the superstition," Chris hissed. He closed his book with a snap and pulled out his pencils and pens. I'd been slowly doing the same. We each placed them neatly on the tables we sat at, looking at Dr. Maitland, the professor.

Dr. Maitland was a round woman with salt and pepper hair and a face that's too kind to teach economics. She only teaches upper-level courses, so perhaps her frown doesn't have to be so pronounced because everyone in her classes actually kind of wants to be here, or else is there because they need to know the information to get to a class they do want.

When she started talking, the little whispered conversations all ceased and we waited for our test. It took me about an hour to finish. I was the third person done. I appreciated the smile Dr. Maitland gave me as she collected my paper.

"Be careful out there," she said.

I noticed one of those fat construction flashlights in her bag. The campus knew something was up. As I headed down the hall, by myself this time, I wondered why they hadn't made sure a Lucia Bride had been crowned despite a lack of ceremony. It seemed like an obvious thing.

Of course, then people would have to admit to believing in superstitions. It might be okay while we were essentially under siege from creatures that roamed the dark, but it was less likely to be okay once things calmed down again.

Yule was December 21st this year. Only six more days until we were all safe.

Or at least until I thought we were all safe.

Two freshmen guys and a freshman girl stood around in the lobby. The girl looked worried. The guys were trying to tell her to call Campus Security to escort her.

"If you're going to the dorms, I'm going that way," I said. Better to walk with someone than no one at all. "Unless you've called Campus Security?"

The girl shook her head. "Not yet. I didn't realize it would be so dark when I finished."

"Take the flashlight, too," the freshman with shaggy blonde hair said. He was clearly interested in the woman waiting. She was pretty in a thin, pale, lifeless sort of way. She gave him a watery smile.

I noticed his pal, with darker hair and eyes, had his own flashlight, though it wasn't one of the huge ones.

"With two of us and a flashlight, we should be good," I said. "Unless you want to walk along?"

Shaggy blonde guy shook his head. "There's something out there."

If he'd added the word "man" I'd have worried he idolized Scooby Do's equally shaggy owner. His pupils were slightly dilated and I figured he was on something. Maybe why the girl wasn't all that interested. Heck, I make no secret of my past, but even I don't use during finals.

As the freshman girl and I set out across campus I looked over at her and asked, "What's your name?"

"Sarah." Her voice was low and quiet in the night. Still, it seemed louder than it should as if the darkness was echoing back our words.

"Mina," I said. I tried to keep my voice low, but again, the sense that something was enhancing our voices remained. My boots had thick rubber soles and now and again they made the faintest squeak that sounded like a scream in the early evening darkness. I winced every time it happened.

Sarah walked quickly. I noticed she threw a longing glance over her shoulder at the cafeteria but she didn't turn. My stomach growled. I'd not eaten as much as I should have at lunch. I knew I'd be eating light at dinner. I had the wings I'd purchased the other day. Jen and I had gotten some bread to spread her peanut butter on too. I also had some carrot sticks in a package to munch on. Plenty to eat, even if it wasn't exactly what I wanted.

A few other women came out of the science building and hurried towards the dorms along with us. We all sort of stayed in a group, coalescing around those who had flashlights. None of us knew each other, though I recognized one of the women from my dorm, but we didn't want to be alone.

The good news was that no shadows attacked us. No monsters reached out to finger our hair. In fact, by the time we got to the quad and the freshman from the business building headed down to the far dorm with two of the other women, my dorm mate and I were almost giggling at our fears.

Until we reached the door and something did tug at her hair. From the corner of my eye, even as my hand reached for the metal handle of the door, I saw a hand, larger than a hand should be, faintly green in the golden light of the lamps that flanked the entryway.

She screamed. I yanked the door open, grabbed her hand, and dragged her inside into the warmth.

A rocky green shape moved into the darkness, the shadow eating the light. My heart beat too fast. My stomach no longer ached for food. Now it ached in fear that I would *be* food.

Nothing followed us inside as the door closed far too slowly. Through the stained glass, I saw shadows dance around on the porch. Fear of what I wasn't seeing made me hurry towards the stairwell, though the woman who had been touched stood in the lobby feeling the back of her neck.

I stopped when I noticed the deep red staining her fingers, and the drops of blood dotting her collar.

Chapter Twelve

The lobby erupted in hysteria. The woman who'd come in with me started to scream. Her earlier scream of terror had brought the desk person from around the desk to see what was going on. The second scream brought a few people running down the stairs and a couple of women from the first floor wings of the dorm.

I had always wished for a first-floor room so that I didn't have to either wait for the elevator to slowly make its way up to the fourth floor or walk up the stairs on my own when I was tired. Suddenly my inconveniences weren't so inconvenient. I wasn't on the floor that would be attacked first if the creatures made their way inside. Granted, I wouldn't have a place to run if they did get inside, but I wouldn't be among the first people killed.

I couldn't say if that was a good thing or not. I mean, yeah I'd live longer but I'd also live knowing what was likely to happen to me.

As other women rushed around me, pulling down my dorm mate's coat collar and looking at the scratches—and they were scratches, thin lines of blood going from her hairline to the edge of her collar from right to left—I stood back and let them surround her.

"You were with her," Claire, the front desk person said, pointing at me.

"We were walking in a group," I said. "Several other women went next door."

"Did you see anything?" Claire demanded. She drew herself up. She was a junior, like me, only she was hoping to be a resident assistant next year. She didn't miss a chance to wrestle down any chance of taking charge. Clearly, she saw this moment as her opportunity to act the heroine.

"It was dark." Which was about the stupidest thing ever said. They all knew it was dark.

"And?" Claire asked. "Those are big scratches. How did you not see something?"

"I didn't look," I said. I wasn't going to admit to seeing a huge hand, one that in my memory was as long as my thigh and slightly green. I could've imagined that I saw thick white claws at the end of the hand instead of nails. Already, my brain had filled in details I couldn't possibly have noticed with the most horrifying additions it could come up with. While I lacked Stephen King's imagination, having read about the darker aspects of the longest night over the last few days, I had plenty of pretty horrifying ideas.

Claire stared at me for a long while. When she had children, because I had no doubt she would someday, Claire would make a formidable mother. Those kids would be squirming under that stare. I've had plenty of time to perfect my non-squirm even under my mom's far more practiced stare, so Claire's look didn't bother me. Even if it had, I wasn't admitting to what I might have seen.

"What she saw or didn't see isn't important," another girl snapped. "We need a first aid kit."

"If it was a bear…" Claire started.

Everyone kind of just turned and looked at her like she was crazy.

Claire sighed and grabbed the kit from behind the desk. "We should call 911 and have someone look at it. Maybe take her to the hospital."

Several of the women in the dorm exchanged glances. "Do you think it's safe?"

The question came from a quiet, dark-haired freshman. Her dark locks tumbled around her face, but though they were thick, they were short, hanging no longer than the tips of her ears.

Claire didn't answer immediately. Then she decided.

"It's not safe to do nothing if we don't know what cut her." She grabbed the desk phone and dialed.

I stayed in the lobby, sliding down into one of the overstuffed chairs angled away from the door. No one sat in it, a surprise considering how comfortable the chair was. An old brown thing that could have come from someone's great grandmother's garage sale, the cushions remained surprisingly soft and cushiony. The thick arms had just the right amount of plush and the fabric was worn to a softness that comes from the sliding of many butts and legs and arms around the material. If it stank ever so slightly, it was a forgivable sin all things considered.

I pulled my backpack around to my front and watched as more people flooded into the lobby. A couple of people volunteered to start cleaning the wound.

My heart calmed to a more normal rate. The surge of adrenaline fast leaving my body made me tired. I hadn't slept well in two nights. Suddenly my eyelids were heavy and I wanted to go upstairs to take a nap. Except I also wanted to know what was happening.

I listened to conversations, most of them about the wounds. We waited to hear sirens. Instead, Campus Security arrived.

"Local paramedics are swamped," the officer said. Sandra. The woman who had escorted me to the security office a few nights ago. Saturday hadn't been that long ago, but life had changed, for me at least, so much. "This was on campus and didn't sound like an immediate threat."

Sandra had another first aid kit, this one bigger, more like a box a paramedic might carry but hers was probably more lightly stocked. Another security officer was with her, holding a flashlight, which he switched off only when the front door had firmly closed, though the stained glass let in the light from the front spotlights.

Half the dorm seemed to have crowded into the lobby and the lounge beyond. Most everyone was standing. Someone decided to make popcorn and soon enough bags were being passed around from person to person, everyone not immediately involved in doing first aid taking a handful and passing it around.

The crunch of the popcorn woke my stomach back up, reminding me I needed to eat. But the chair was comfortable and I had hope of more popcorn soon enough.

Everyone was talking, discussing what they'd seen. Lots of odd shadows. A few strange creatures that looked like something out of a particularly nasty version of the Brothers Grimm. One woman was certain she'd seen a dragon flying over Lake Superior.

I discounted the last one as just reaching for attention. Maybe because dragons didn't seem like they'd be creatures of the night. For all their fantastic powers, they wouldn't need to hide in the shadows.

"It's because there's no Lucia Bride," someone whispered.

"Maybe we should crown one," I suggested from my chair, not turning around to see who was speaking.

"That's a perfect idea!" I recognized Naomi's voice.

The idea took hold as the women in my dorm all discussed the logistics of what would need to be done to crown Lucia Bride when it wasn't the thirteenth. The noise died abruptly when something banged on the front window, hard.

The sound had me leaping out of the chair. With all the lights on, I couldn't see a thing but the three women who had pressed their faces to the glass drew back in a scream just as whatever was out there pounded against the glass once more.

Chapter Thirteen

The pounding thundered through the lounge and lobby. The women in the lobby backed up into the lounge. A few headed upstairs, whether to hide in their rooms or to watch from the lounges higher up, I didn't know. I backed away from the chair, getting closer to the stairs myself. Not yet ready to leave, because I wanted to see what I was facing.

Well, I didn't exactly want to see what I was facing, but the old saying better a devil you know suddenly seemed appropriate. If I knew it was solid and toothy, I could run from that. If it was amorphous and shadowy, that would be harder to fight. I didn't want to be alone with a creature like that.

Several girls started to cry even as they huddled together. The girls remaining were like a herd of animals, crowding together shoulder to shoulder, the ones on the edges facing outward, forming a wall against intruders, protecting the injured in the center.

Nothing broke through the front door, despite its glass. Nothing banged on the windows now that nearly everyone had left the lounge and certainly no one stood around near the windows eating popcorn and drinking sodas.

The silence stretched, broken only by the occasional whimper. Upstairs someone moved in their room and the ceiling creaked. All heads looked up to see if something were hanging on the ceiling, including mine, though I knew it was foolish. Nothing was up there. Nothing could get in.

I tried to focus on my breathing. Someone started to hyperventilate. That started tears and even a few small screams. The waiting and the noise had a few others fleeing up the stairs. So much for solidarity.

I wanted to join those fleeing, but upstairs only my dark and empty room awaited. Shadows would lurk in corners no matter how many lights I turned on and faces might appear at windows, could perhaps even look through the blinds and see a woman alone, terrified. My room offered no comfort. Here, perhaps I could learn something about the night terror I faced.

Once again, I talked myself into remaining in the lobby.

I tuned into the murmurs of conversation swirling around me. No one was talking about crowning a new Lucia Bride. I pulled out my phone and leaned against the wall next to the stairs. A prime location. I started searching through information on St. Lucia and the Lucia Bride Ceremony. Nothing talked about who had to crown her or if there was something special about the girl chosen.

They had to represent the qualities of St. Lucia which included service to others, strength of character, leadership, and compassion. I mulled over whether the woman or girl actually had to be crowned. Apparently, sophomore girls were always chosen because St. Lucia was supposed to be just twenty when she was martyred. Strange how legends and superstitions grow.

Lucia was supposed to bring light to the darkness and food to the poor. Still nothing about who crowned her or how she had to be chosen. She had to be recognized by her peers, though. All the ceremonies recognized her.

"I can't find anything on choosing a particular Lucia Bride," I said to the crowd which continued to ignore me, intent upon their own small conversations. "I think we just have to decide on someone and recognize her."

"And then what?" one of the women on the first floor demanded. "Do we send her out with a crown of candles and food and let her get killed by those things out there?"

"I haven't gotten that far yet," I said. "I mean most years we don't send the Lucia Bride out to battle monsters. Just her presence prevents them from appearing, right?"

The woman who didn't like my plan continued to shut down my comments, snapping away at me with her logic. I closed my phone and continued to lean back against the wall, listening.

Some of the girls wanted to crown someone and hope that just by crowning someone the creatures would go away. Even amongst themselves, those girls were arguing about who needed to vote and how to choose. I didn't offer any further input.

I wasn't being a sore loser.

Really.

I wanted to know what other people were thinking. I honestly didn't know what to do next.

"I think that's as clean as we can get it," Sandra from Campus Security said.

A huge bandage covered the back of the girl's neck, her hair pulled up in a clip so that Sandra could do her work.

"We should go," the male security person said. He picked up his heavy flashlight and glanced around, eyes worried. He didn't want to go out. I didn't blame him.

Sandra picked up her security radio and started talking into it. I couldn't make out everything, but it sounded like students were waiting to be escorted from the cafeteria to their dorms, both women and men. Several people had heard screams around campus and those were being investigated. One of the pairs of officers hadn't been heard from in five minutes and they wanted someone to go to check their last known location.

"We're between the dorms and the cafeteria, so we'll head that way first," Sandra said.

She took the large first aid kit that was probably a weapon all on its own and headed towards the door, pausing to be sure her companion was with her. He'd already turned on the large light. He swallowed twice, his Adam's apple bobbing hard in his throat, and followed Sandra out into the night.

I saw nothing out there, only the pools of light left by the outdoor lights at the entrance, a safe puddle of white before the darkness tried swallowing it. The flashlight was bright as it carved away a lighted path to the little golf cart the security people had used to travel around campus.

The door closed behind them and I was left in the dorm with the other women who were all as terrified as I was.

"Where's Jen?" Naomi asked, crossing the room to me. She wiped her eyes. She'd been one of the women crying.

"Her mom came for her. They're in a hotel in town," I said.

"And she didn't take you?" Naomi asked.

I shook my head.

"So you're alone in your room?"

"Looks that way," I said.

Naomi nodded. "This scares me. I wish my finals were over and I could just leave. In the morning, I mean. So far, no one's been killed in a building."

"The legends I've read says that people are safe in buildings." I stood up straight. While some of the women stayed in the lobby, more were filing out as their wounded friend went to her room to rest.

"But I think people were supposed to keep their doors and windows locked," Naomi said. "An unlocked door…" she trailed off looking at our door. The door would be locked at ten. Until then there would be someone at the desk. Not that being at the desk seemed like a good place to be.

"We can lock our room doors," I said.

"No bathroom—and that door doesn't lock," Naomi whispered. As if someone would listen in and get an idea. Her thoughts only echoed mine and offered nothing new for me to consider as we slowly climbed the stairs to our wing.

"At least we're on the fourth floor," I said. "I would think that if something came through the door, it would stay on the lower floor."

"Unless it likes our ghost," Naomi said.

I glanced at her, wondering if she was joking. Supposedly there was a ghost on the other wing of the fourth floor. One of the first women admitted to the college in 1943 had killed herself. Rumor had it she'd been in love with someone and he'd left her alone and pregnant, and she'd decided death was better than the disgrace. Other rumors suggested she'd been a victim of rape.

There was little information other than the fact that a girl had committed suicide in that wing in 1943. Lots of women swore they saw her walking down the hall to the stairs. Others said they saw her crying. Her room was now the kitchen, which was in the middle of the hallway instead of at the end like the other kitchens. Sometimes it was said she could be seen standing near the window looking out.

The only credence I gave was that they'd made a kitchen in a different place on that wing than they had on any other wing of the dorm. Someone had felt or seen something. Or else someone early on couldn't force others to sleep in a room where someone had died and had changed the configuration. As a result, the room on that end of the dorm on the fourth floor held three girls and was larger than any other room in the building.

Being in the haunted dorm when there were monsters outside didn't thrill me. At least I wasn't next door to where the ghost had been seen. I was really glad I didn't have to walk down that hall during the night to use the bathroom.

Right about then, I was wishing I'd gotten assigned to the top floor. Of course, someone had mentioned dragons. They weren't the only flying creatures out there. My imagination went to the flying monkeys that worked for Oz's Wicked Witch of the West. My wingmate Kennedy's love for the movie probably playing into that. Monkeys could probably open a window. Maybe the top floor was less than desirable.

"I heard that there was a guy on the edge of town found dead out near his mailbox this morning," I told Naomi.

She nodded. "Someone told me that too. It's not just the school. It's the whole town. I called my mom yesterday to see how things were and she said that it had been a busy night for the police. She heard sirens all over the place. I asked her to stay in after dark. Fortunately, my dad's company has a big parking garage where he parks, and then he can pull into the garage at home so he's not walking around outside, really."

I didn't mention that most parking garages were not completely enclosed unless they were in a basement. Maybe her dad's was like that. Even so, maybe a big structure was less desirable to creatures that had hands the size of my thighs. I mean how would they fit? I'd seen plenty of smaller creatures, too, but perhaps they weren't as dangerous.

Remembering the long sharp teeth I'd seen in the face at the window, I doubted there was anything out there that wasn't dangerous.

I thought about my parents. Wisconsin was a whole lot closer to Minnesota than North Carolina. Were they also hearing lots of sirens in the night? Was my dad safe walking from his office to his car or from the driveway to our front door? My parents used their garage for things other than parking the car, so he didn't have that latter safety that Naomi's father had.

"Do they know what's going on?" I asked. I hoped that perhaps Naomi had a tactful way of getting information from her parents so I could call my own and check. I have my issues with them, but I had no desire to have them murdered by strange night beasts that seemed to have no reason for existence other than murdering humans.

Naomi shook her head. "Only that something is up. They know that I saw a body here. My mom isn't happy that I want to stay for finals, but all the flights with available seats leave after dark."

Even taking a plane, I wouldn't want to leave after dark, either. I thought about getting back home to an airport that was mostly closed but for the people on my flight. I thought about dark parking garages and darkened shops and restaurants, empty gates. While lights might be on, it would be even more lonely in those spaces than here, where at least I had a bunch of people who all at least half-believed in the monsters out there.

Reaching our floor, Naomi and I headed down the hallway. I stopped in the bathroom. It was on the way. Maybe I could wait until morning to leave my room again. Or at least until I heard someone else moving around.

Back in my room, I locked the door and made sure all the blinds were closed. The place felt particularly empty without Jen. My mattress was back on my bed. I wished she were still there so we could have huddled together and both gotten at least a little sleep, safe in the knowledge that if the worst happened we wouldn't die alone.

I settled in with my laptop and started reading more about Lucia Bride and the longest night. I leaned back, wondering what things might stop the monsters during the darkness.

Lucia Bride was celebrated on December 13 instead of the solstice because the festival had been placed on an earlier calendar when the thirteenth was the longest night. When the calendar had changed, the date stayed the same. Night monsters wouldn't care about specific dates. They'd care about the darkness.

Longer nights might mean longer dreams, at least historically. Ghosts, I learned were often memories of people embedded in the places they haunted. Monsters could be like that, too. The origin of the issue was the burning of the church. I hadn't been by there since the fire. I had an afternoon final but it was earlier than economics. I'd walk over to the church and search for clues in the morning.

I didn't think there was much I could do that evening so I settled in to try and focus on my studies for the next day.

I calmed enough to eat the wings I'd purchased and some of the vegetable sticks. I didn't drink anything with caffeine because I worried about being able to sleep. The dorm around me settled in, though the normal sounds weren't quite the same.

No music floated up to my room. No laughter pierced the night when two people met up and told a particularly good joke. Instead, toilets flushed one after the other. Water flooded through pipes for handwashing. A group of women would walk down a hallway together.

I longed for a roommate to hold my hand as I hurried to the bathroom. Jen was lucky to be in a hotel, but hiding away wouldn't make the problems stop. Everyone assumed that they'd end on the solstice, or Yule, because that's what legends said would happen. I worried that the legends might be wrong.

Chapter Fourteen

I woke the next morning after a night of poor sleep, though there were only minimal scares. Something banged on the window at one point which kept me up for about an hour. After that, I heard someone coming out of the room catty-corner across the hall from us. Peering out, I saw it was just one of my neighbors heading to the bathroom. As my bladder had been demanding attention, I hurried out after them. Safety in numbers, after all.

Though the full hall lights had been left on even past eleven, the dark still crept up around the edges, threatening to plunge us into inky blackness at any moment. Shadows skittered though I saw nothing to have caused the movement. Perhaps it was my imagination but after my experiences the last few nights, I wasn't counting on it. Small creatures might have slipped inside when the crowd had been in the lobby and hidden in the corners where light never seemed to penetrate.

As I hurried down the hall, I was glad I didn't have laundry that needed doing. The washers and dryers existed in the basement with only one large window that opened out to an egress that had been dug into the ground. Around back, cellar stairs descended to a fire door, locked to the outside world, but opening from the inside. A safety thing.

Creatures of the darkness would adore the basements of this building. Darkness hovered there at the best of times, and the old furnace creaked and groaned loudly enough to cover all but the loudest footsteps. Washers and driers whirred and hummed, though I doubted anyone was eager to be down there. I had seen more than the usual amount of underwear hand-washed in the bathroom sinks.

Mine could wait until I got home to the laundry room at home, which was on the first floor. With a bright light.

After scaring myself during my walk to the bathroom, I found it hard to get back to sleep. Still, as this was the second night of poor sleep, I did finally drift off, waking only after it was full light. I hurried down the hall to the bathroom and showered. I wanted to have time to wander around at the church before going to lunch.

No one waited in the lobby, though I noticed that the sofa closest to the window had been moved to the middle of the room. The lights remained on, though daylight filtered in, and normally a light wouldn't be needed. A different desk worker kept an eye on the front door, her face more serious than usual.

Gray clouds continued to hang low in the sky. Less fog curled beneath bushes and at the base of the buildings. Thin snow still covered the ground, but the day didn't smell as if more would be coming. The white blanket, thin though it was, made the outdoors brighter, though the gray clouds did their best to minimize that light.

My breath fogged the air when I stepped outside. I

walked quickly away from the dorm, my backpack a solid weight against my back, protecting it from an attack should one come from behind. A few other women were out and about, mostly hurrying to other buildings, perhaps for finals, perhaps to eat or to work.

Once again I wished I had a better sense of how finals worked at HLC or anywhere but PLU. Winter finals at St. Lucy's had been disrupted by the disciplinary committee meetings after the Lucia Bride incident. That week had been a blur of stress-related nightmares and vows to never sell to students I didn't know really well ever again.

Inside the math building, I noted staff moving around behind windows lit with bright lights. Shadows waved outside the windows, but these were the normal shadows of trees moving in a light breeze that brought a chill even through my winter jacket.

I kept my hands in my pockets and my head down. A couple of times I waved at people I knew slightly. The campus was definitely quiet for nearing midday on only the second day of finals.

When I reached the church, I looked at the building. It had been rounded rather than rectangular, though not quite a dome in shape. The narrow entrance that stuck out like the gangplank of a ship was undamaged but for one small area of blackened wood.

Broken glass lay scattered near the edges of the building though not nearly as much as I'd have expected. I'd have to watch where I walked going closer. Not all pieces of glass would have landed neatly on their sides. Some would have dug their sharp edges into the dirt, their upper edges waiting to gouge unsuspecting walkers.

The ramp to the entry of the church held little snow. Though it hadn't burned, it might have remained too warm for the snow to stick there. A bare area at least three feet wide surrounded that side of the church. Stones had fallen away, some on the ground, some inside the church just to the left of the gangplank entrance. I paused looking up the ramp, trying to see how damaged it was and what I could see of the church from my vantage at the base.

The way the church had burned left a wide hole for me to look through. Even from there, it was apparent that the interior was no longer covered in red carpet and blonde wood pews to match the altar as I recalled from photos. Now, the walls to the blank-eyed window frames were blackened. The red carpet was stained burgundy in the spaces where it wasn't gone completely.

The church was a complete loss. Had it contained something to protect the town, I didn't know how I'd find it.

I glanced around. There were homes on the other side of the street, but no one seemed to be in the front rooms. All the front windows were dark with curtains and blinds closed, though one had dim lights, probably from the back of the house. I walked closer to the church, picking my way carefully.

I noted the posted "Keep Out" and "Danger Signs" stapled to various burnt timbers. Two others that defined trespassing, were posted at the edges of the property. Nothing in front of the gangplank entrance, which seemed like the obvious place to put something. Maybe someone else had been here and taken it.

I didn't go all the way into the building. I'm not a complete idiot. Several large holes gaped in the floor of the church, nearest to the altar. The angle of the shadows suggested that the church had been built above a basement. So did the way the gangplank entry angled up.

Though the gangplank was open to the air, there was a cover over the top and most of that was intact, keeping things darker than they had been on the street.

I stretched my neck as far as I could, but nothing stood out. I went back down the ramp. I'd have to go around the back to see if I could see an entrance to the basement, or perhaps get closer to the altar to look down into the basement.

Snow covered the rest of what had once been a parking lot. If the church hadn't burned, no doubt the lot would have been plowed. I walked slowly and carefully, placing my feet only when I had made sure there were no shards of glass sticking up. If anything didn't crunch down easily beneath my boots I moved back to where I'd been standing. I hated leaving footprints as a sign of my passing but there was no help for it.

I made my way around the building and into the grass that lay between the trees and the church. The naked gray tree branches blended into the gray skies above my head. Light trails of snow covered most of the branches. Evergreen bushes huddled beneath the naked branches, absorbing as much sun as they could before spring let the trees once again leaf out and shade them.

The back of the church looked worse than the front. Most of the wood was blackened and parts of the roof had caved in. A few timbers leaned at drunken angles to each other and looked as if they could fall over at a moment's notice.

I paused, wondering how to get closer. The windows were above my head and although the upper walls were burnt out, the lower part of the building was all brick and held nothing I could look through.

Behind me, something moved. Every cell in my body screamed run. I glanced down, noting the shiny pieces of glass that lay partially buried in the snow. I couldn't move quickly there. Still, I backed up, hoping to reach the cover of the trees before someone, or worse, *something*, found me.

I didn't make it. Before I'd taken three steps, a warmly dressed man came around the corner. His head was covered in one of those fur caps that I'd always associated with Russia. Earflaps covered his ears. Stray dark hairs stuck out from the edges nearest his face. His eyes were sharp behind thick wire-rimmed glasses that were smaller than was fashionable.

I paused in my movements. At least whoever this was, he was human and wasn't a police officer. The police wore black jackets that reached mid-thigh. This man wore a charcoal gray wool coat that fell just below his knees, though he wasn't a short man. Heavy black boots reached nearly to the hem of the coat.

"What are you doing here?" he asked. His voice wasn't loud nor was it angry sounding. Maybe a hint of a song in the tones of his voice, as if he were more used to singing than speaking.

"I was looking around," I said, trying not to stammer too much. Explaining that I was looking at the church for clues to where the monsters might have come from didn't seem politic and anything else seemed suspicious even to my mind. Or perhaps particularly to my mind.

He nodded. "It's not a safe place to wander."

"I noticed the glass," I said. "I was being careful. And I wasn't too close to the building." Of course, I wanted to be, but he didn't need to know that.

"There are worse things than glass," he said.

I waited, hoping he'd clarify.

Nothing. Some detective I'd be. Not only do I not ask the right questions, I am apparently not one of those people that others just open up to like in the old-lady-solves-a-crime type mysteries my mom reads.

"You should get back to your school and your finals," he said. "It was bold of you to come here, to look around. Answers aren't here, though. They're inside."

"Inside the church?" I asked. I mentally slapped myself. I'd given away my plan or my thoughts. Now he'd think I was crazy, though it seemed that he, too, believed something was going on.

He smiled at me. I've heard the term radiant smile and when he smiled, I felt I finally understood that term. It wasn't that he was so happy. It was just peaceful and knowing and put me at ease.

"No. Not that inside," he said. His smile vanished. "But you were smart to go looking. It might be daytime but the clouds hang thick and night will come sooner than expected. Remain safe, for those who are bold and brave in searching for answers are noticed, and not all that notice you are kind."

I had no idea what to say to that. He was probably the pastor of the church and used to talking in strange riddles and metaphors. I avoided church when I could and zoned out when I couldn't. He seemed like a good guy, though, the sort of person I might listen to if I had to sit in a pew while he delivered a sermon.

I walked carefully away from the back of the church, following my trail back around the front. The street remained quiet.

I glanced at my phone checking to see how much more time I had. I could grab lunch and make it to my next final without a problem. I glanced back but didn't see the pastor coming around the front. He was probably checking to make sure I hadn't damaged anything.

I shook my head and continued my walk, less frightened than I'd been earlier, though nothing had really changed. I would still spend the evening terrified in my room. Alone. But somehow, speaking to the pastor had calmed me in some strange way. Until I realized, halfway back to the campus, that I hadn't seen a single trace of any footprints besides my own.

Chapter Fifteen

Twilight raced in while I took my afternoon final. The fog had returned as well, turning the campus into a mysterious cloud world that looked nothing like it normally did. This fog didn't just circle and wait near the bushes and the edges of buildings. This fog blinded you, stranding you alone in the world, cutting you off from all that you knew.

Fog didn't normally obscure the world during the winter. It happened more as the temperatures fluctuated and clouds dropped rain, but it wasn't completely unheard of. Just not quite normal like everything else.

I had no desire to step out into that gray non-world but I pulled out my phone and turned on my flashlight app. Fortunately, there were other people in the building taking finals and the dorms weren't far. Besides, the twilight was gray, not black, though I worried about the creatures slipping through the foggy shadows. The pastor's words came back to me about night falling sooner than expected. The fog and the limited vision worked much like night. The creatures could be out.

The sounds of the other women walking out the door

were muffled by the dampness of the air. While no one talked much, each of us feeling less than certain about our world when we couldn't see it, the sounds of boots on the cobbles, the scuffing of snow when someone walked off the path and onto the grass, even a cough, all sounded wrong. Distances were hard to estimate.

I heard someone sneeze, but they weren't part of our group. It seemed like forever before someone walking the other direction, hurrying along with another woman in tow, passed us, a trembling smile on their face. I did not envy them their schedule.

I waited to feel something against the back of my neck, though there were women behind me. I strained to hear the faintest of screams or muffled grunts or groans but nothing reached me. I didn't even hear the faint sounds of the small creatures that often roamed campus. No cars drove by a few streets away, or if they did, they were dreamily silent.

The world had fled from Havestad. I didn't blame it. Perhaps there were places where life went on normally.

I turned down the walk that should have taken me to the dorm, though I could make out only a shadow in that direction. I made the walk that felt longer than it had even the night before in the dark, fleeing from something I didn't quite see. Still, eventually, the dorm appeared in front of me.

One moment fog surrounded me. The next, the building waited, lights burning from every room. The blinds in the lounge had been opened. I wondered if they would remain that way.

I slipped in through the door which was unlocked. The desk worker greeted me. Allyson. I knew her slightly. Business major. Blonde. She was from North Dakota.

"Some weather," she said, looking up. I thought I saw her eyebrows pull together for a moment.

"I'll say," I said. "This isn't really typical winter weather, at least not at home."

Allyson shook her head. "Not at my home either. Nor are the night creatures."

The answers were inside, the pastor had said. Perhaps Allyson had answers for me. She was, after all, inside the building. This was inside. I could look there.

"I'd never heard of night creatures before. I've definitely never had to practically run across campus to avoid getting attacked," I said. I glanced over my shoulder when another girl came in. She waved at Allyson and hurried to the stairwell.

"I don't think anyone has," Allyson said. She looked down at the desk before looking back up at me. "It's really weird. I mean, I've heard the Lussi legends and the dark night but they were just legends. My mom said there've been three murders in town and no one knows how the people were killed. One could have been killed by a bear but the others didn't have a mark on them, just fallen down on the sidewalk, both of them, together. It's creeping me out. I get into the airport at night."

"I don't envy you," I said. I was glad I drove. Glad I only had a five-plus hour drive. I could leave as the sun came up and then be home well before dark, safely ensconced in the house where I planned to stay until the solstice.

"My mom doesn't believe it's just Lussi the witch. I mean that was a completely different legend than St. Lucia. She thinks there's something else going on."

"Like?" I asked. Answers, the pastor had said.

"She didn't know," Allyson said. "She thought perhaps something burning down the church on St. Lucia Day let creatures loose or maybe there was something special about the church."

"I went to the church," I said. "But I think I ran into the pastor and had to leave."

Allyson frowned. "It couldn't have been the pastor."

Dread filled me. "Why not?"

"They found him in the basement just last night. It was the first time they could get inside to do a full walk-through. They found a body and the pastor has been missing, so they're sure it's him. He wasn't a young man. No one knows why he went down there or what he did, but they're pretty sure he died in the fire, not before. It's one reason my mother is all gung ho that there's something wrong because the church burned down," Allyson said.

"I wonder if the man I saw was affiliated with the church some other way. He seemed very pastoral." I had no idea if pastoral was an appropriate word in this context. Allyson didn't seem to notice.

She nodded. "I understand the type. Maybe one of our campus ministers."

I nodded. I'd seen both ministers around campus. One was a woman. The other was a much older man than the person I'd run into. I slipped up the stairs, not liking the answers I seemed to be getting from Allyson.

The answers are inside. Yeah. I'd had answers. Too bad they weren't helpful answers and just brought up more questions.

Chapter Sixteen

I struggled to study anything that evening as the sky got darker and darker. The blinds remained closed from earlier in the day. It's not like I had spent much awake time in the room earlier.

Before night had fully fallen, I heard loud hoots outside. I am not unfamiliar with owls but I'd never heard anything that loud. An owl might have been hooting into a megaphone three feet from my ears. I heard doors opening out into the hall and people asking if others had heard the sounds.

"Heard it," I said when I came out of my room. Dinner smells from the kitchen reached me, an assortment of soups and quickly heated TV dinners. Considering how many people appeared to be eating in right then, I was glad Jen and I had hit the grocery store early.

Cassidy and Kennedy, the two women across the hall were out in the hall, Kennedy in her red "Dorothy" slippers. Dee and Wendy from next door peeked their heads out, the kitchen between us. Marble and Lori were a few doors down in what I saw as a now envied position of directly across the hallway from the bathroom. Marble was already in pajamas, but half the time she went to class in flannel pajama bottoms. It was only when it started to get cooler that she started putting on clothing, which usually consisted of sweatpants.

Cassidy flipped her black hair, streaked with teal, and clearly ironed flat, over her shoulder. "I don't know how anyone could miss it. We ought to have a meeting. Where's Rebecca?"

The resident assistant assigned to our wing was a senior named Rebecca, who was much too serious and tended to stay holed up in her room more than any RA I'd had in all my years of school. At PLU, the RA had been made it a point to talk to every single one of us every single day, at least to say hello to and to make sure we were all okay. At St. Lucy's the Wing Monitor as they were called there, made it a point to get everyone together once a month to discuss what was going on in everyone's lives and ran the whole process like she was running a group therapy session. I'd gone to two, the second only because I'd forgotten it was happening and was practically dragged out of my room.

Rebecca had a heavier class load than she'd expected and spent a fair amount of time studying in the library. I tried to remember the last time I'd seen her. She'd not been in the lobby yesterday, I knew that. I hadn't seen her at all at night.

Everyone shrugged.

Lori hurried down the hall towards the swinging doors that opened onto the upstairs lounge area. Rebecca's room was closest to those in a smaller sized room tucked back from the hallway a bit. Lori disappeared into the vestibule area. I heard her knock, just as the giant owl hooted again.

Upstairs I heard some screams. The fifth-floor girls heard it too.

Lori waited but Rebecca didn't answer. Coming back down the hall, she shrugged. "Maybe at dinner?"

"In which case, she didn't get the memo that we shouldn't be out at night," Cassidy commented.

Kennedy nodded. Where Cassidy was tall and what my mother would call full-figured, Kennedy was shorter and build more like a boy. Cassidy's hair was long and always styled nicely. Cassidy liked to talk and would make a great RA in her senior year. Kennedy was quiet and shy and mostly all I knew about her was that she loved the Wizard of Oz. Kennedy tended to agree with whatever Cassidy said, quietly and behind the scenes.

"Was there a memo?" Marble asked. "We just decided it was too scary last night."

Cassidy rolled her eyes. Nothing official had gone out. A figure of speech that things weren't safe out there.

"Campus Security has been walking people around and giving rides," I said. "She could be fine."

The giant owl hoot echoed through the hall again. The sounds came from everywhere around me. I felt as if I was surrounded by a giant ghost owl I couldn't quite see. I imagined the shadows coalescing into wings and a beak.

"It sounds closer," Marble said. "I don't like this. I wish finals were over."

"My dad is worried. He heard that creatures were sneaking through gardens and peeping in windows last night. And that was at home, not here," Cassidy said. She lived in a suburb of Minneapolis.

Peeping and sneaking were one thing. I wondered if other people had died. It might be harder to hear about from a city like Minneapolis. It was so much larger and would likely have more crime to begin with. A few night creatures adding to it, wouldn't be as noticeable as they were in smaller places.

Lori rubbed her arms.

We all jumped when the door at the end of the hall banged open. Rebecca appeared.

"I just came back from an RA meeting in the dorm," she said. "The cafeteria will be closing at lunchtime. They'll be packing up box dinners for those who want to take them when they come through for lunch. We can't reschedule all finals to the mornings, but we can keep people from going out for anything else. All dorms will lock up the front door at six-thirty instead of eleven. Everyone is asked to stay in their rooms as much as possible."

Rebecca gave us all a hard look as if we were deliberately breaking a rule we should have known about.

The owl hooted again.

Rebecca jumped slightly.

"It's getting worse each night," she said. "And while it's the worst here, it's not just local."

So tell us something we didn't know. I hoped I wasn't glaring at her when she spoke. I wanted answers.

"Does anyone know what we can do about this?" I asked.

Everyone turned to look at me. Apparently, everyone else just assumed we'd ride it out, waiting for someone else to figure things out rather than doing anything.

Rebecca gave me a long look. She opened her mouth once and closed it. Then she finally gathered her thoughts. "What exactly do you think we can do? No one even knows what these things are. I realize not everyone believes in ghosts and crap. I certainly don't, but these things appear to defy science. If this is a huge prank, then the police need to be involved and you need to stay out of it."

"And if it's not a prank?" I asked. "If it's not human?"

The stares suggested that my wingmates all thought I'd lost my mind. Well, all except maybe Kennedy who was nodding along, but she could have been just being agreeable lest I turn on her or something.

"Well, if you're suddenly some supernatural expert, then you go out and take your wooden stakes and find the monster or maybe use your silver bullets but only once you're off-campus. No guns, remember?" Rebecca said. Her voice was low and harsh, harsher than I'd ever heard it and I have a way of annoying people.

I shrugged.

Lori covered her mouth to stop from giggling. Really, whatever I'd said wasn't that funny. Given the way her shoulders were shaking I started thinking she was getting hysterical. Marble drew her inside the room and closed their door. I heard laughter once it was closed, but not Lori's normal laugh. Definitely a level of hysteria.

Cassidy turned to go back to their room. I moved quietly towards my room.

"Mina," Rebecca called.

I turned and looked back at her.

"Don't get yourself killed trying to play Dr. Van Helsing, okay?"

I smiled a little and returned to the relative safety of my room just as the owl hooted again. Someone pounded on the floor upstairs making me worry the owl had eaten through the roof and gotten in. Then I heard the soft murmurs of voices talking.

I didn't feel very hungry and my room, which always felt so small with Jen and me, suddenly felt far too large. My sleeping cubby was no longer a nice little cubby to crawl into for privacy but a shadowed area where something might hide. Jen's was worse because there was no one to occupy it.

The school was closing the cafeteria. People had died. They knew something, something I didn't know. Or maybe they just thought they knew something.

The answers, the pastor who was not the church pastor said, were inside, but not inside the church. There'd been more questions than answers in the dorm. I was missing something.

Chapter Seventeen

The mysterious creature that sounded like an owl continued hooting at an irregular rate. I managed to almost fall asleep twice only to be woken by the sounds of it hooting again. I huddled under the blankets, my heart pounding too hard, waiting for another sound that didn't come.

I'd gradually calm my breathing and close my eyes. My heart rate would slow down. I'd drift away and the owl would hoot again. I wondered how many of my dorm mates were on nearly the same drift-off schedule I was. I think I managed five minutes of sleep, once.

I envied anyone who had an afternoon final on Wednesday. At least they'd get some sleep. Business law started at 10. I barely made it.

Everyone else in the room looked as haggard as I felt, even the guys. The mysterious sounds had clearly not just tormented and tortured our dorm. And torture it was. I had read about sleep deprivation. At least the creatures were gone during the day.

The final was a blur. It had a long section of multiple

choice and fill in the blanks which would probably give me a passing grade, so maybe I would get that A or an A-. The two final essay questions were more difficult and I hoped that most of my sentences were coherent enough that I would get enough points to maintain that possible A.

I dragged myself across campus to the cafeteria where I ate lunch, a large one, and picked up my box dinner, which was a big sandwich, a salad with my choice of dressing on the side, a bag of chips, a couple of carrot sticks with ranch, and a peanut butter cookie. The latter looked like the best part.

I wasn't going to complain as I could always eat. If I were up late again, I might need a third meal. I dropped my stuff in my dorm room, intent upon taking a nap. I'd curled up and gotten perhaps an hour of sleep when I started awake to the sounds of the room door opening. Normally, I would have slept through such a sound but after the last few nights, I was sleeping much more lightly.

"Who?" I asked, sitting up.

"Just me," Jen said coming into the room. She had her backpack. Her eyes were gray hollows.

"What's up?"

"I came back after my final," she said. "My mom and I are leaving in the morning, at least I hope we are. We hardly got any sleep. There was some sort of growling animal outside the hotel that sounded like it was roaming the halls or something."

"It was an owl here," I said. "I don't think I got more than about five minutes of sleep. I know I didn't study."

"I didn't get much sleep either. I spent the night searching for information on my phone. My mom was up doing some searches as well. I read that the pastor of the church died in the fire." Jen had her phone out as if to demonstrate how she'd searched for information.

"I heard," I said. "I saw someone at the church, though, when I went over there."

"You went there?" Jen's eyes got big.

I nodded. "I thought what if it isn't about Lucia Bride but something about the church fire. I was going to look inside, but there wasn't a way to get in. I met up with some pastor. He said that the answers were inside, but not the church."

Jen frowned. "I can't imagine who would be there. Do you think it was a police officer?"

"I hadn't seen this guy around before. I thought he was the pastor of the church. He just seemed like the kind of person who would be a pastor." I remembered back to the conversation. I couldn't remember if he'd said something that suggested he was the pastor or if I'd just assumed based on the way he walked and talked.

Jen made a face. "That's weird. It sounds like some ghostly figure pointing the way in a movie."

I laughed. She was right though. Or maybe something out of my imagination. That idea niggled at me. I tried to focus on it but nothing came to me.

"What brought you back?" I asked.

"I wanted to say goodbye until next term and that I'm sorry. I know that no matter how bad it was for me in the hotel, it was probably worse here," Jen said. "Plus, I forgot my favorite socks. I had planned to wear them for luck today so had put them in a special place to make sure I didn't actually wear them too soon." She giggled at that.

She had a pair of red and black socks with rabbits on them. She called them her lucky rabbit's feet. She always wore them for any test she was worried about.

"You know, maybe it would have been good if that man had been a pastor. After all, he's a spiritual guide and this seems like something of the spirit, don't you think?"

Jen asked. She pulled the socks out and stuffed them in her backpack. I didn't know why she'd be doing that. She had no more finals.

"Did you really need your socks?" I asked as she did that.

Jen sighed. "It was my excuse to my mom. I do love these socks and I hated leaving them here, but I was hoping to see a few people to talk to before leaving tomorrow. Mom wants to get home as soon as possible. She even considered driving to Duluth this afternoon but I talked her out of it. Could you imagine getting stuck on that road?"

All I could think of were the tall trees and light traffic. It would be a nightmare. Tomorrow, they'd have plenty of daylight. Maybe I'd do the same after my last final. I could just get out of here and stay in a hotel in Duluth, but I didn't trust my luck on the road. What if my car broke down? I really just wanted to hide in the dorms until this was all over. Jen left and I rolled over to try and get back to sleep.

I didn't, though. I kept thinking about what she said about consulting a pastor. I'd never talked to anyone in campus ministry before. Perhaps it was time to start. Perhaps I could get a sense of how this should end. Or maybe they'd at least help me work out the niggling sense of what was tugging at my mind when Jen and I had talked about imagination.

Chapter Eighteen

The campus was looking more and more deserted every time I went out. Some people were done with finals and had left. Others were just holed up in their dorms until they had to go out. The skies remained as gray as ever, though there was less fog today than there had been yesterday. Small cotton candy puffs of the fog remained curled around the buildings and bushes. On a happier day, the campus could have been a perfect picture for winter. Instead, it felt more like a setting for Halloween.

Campus ministry was on the edge of the campus that faced Trinity Lane. The building it was in looked like a cream-colored bungalow. A sign in front listed Campus Ministry, Alumni Office, and Media Relations. When I climbed the wooden stairs to the covered porch which lined the entire front of the building, I noted another sign next to the door. According to that, Campus Ministry took up the first floor and the other two offices were upstairs.

I put my hand on the gold handle, one of those long handles with a thumb press, and paused before opening it. I needed to watch the time. Daylight had yet to disappear and I had at least an hour before dusk arrived, longer before full dark even with the clouds. The upper part of the door was divided into four small panes of glass.

Inside, the hardwood floor was finished in dark wood. Stepping inside, the wide planks of wood on the floor suggested it was no longer original. To my left was an open door to campus ministries. An arrow pointed up the stairwell to the other offices. A bright, modern-looking chandelier hung in the tall entry.

I walked slowly towards the campus ministry offices. The woman sitting at the front desk looked like Pastor Erin. She'd spoken at student orientation which I'd been required to attend even if I wasn't a freshman.

"Can I help you?" she said, crossing her arms on the desk and leaning forward as if helping me was the most important thing in the world.

"Kinda weirded out about this stuff going on," I said. "I mean… I guess I'm not really all that religious, but this makes me wish I was?" I wasn't sure that was honest. It had threads of honesty and, if I were willing to look more closely at my feelings, maybe more than threads.

Erin's short dark hair was neatly combed. Everything about her was tidy, from her heavy cream sweater with black stitching around the collar to the way her eyebrows lined evenly over her face. Even her response was tidy. No laugh, but no frown of judgment either.

"I'm kind of surprised you're the first person to come by with such concerns," Erin said quietly. "Are you okay talking here or do you want to go into my office. Technically, I'm supposed to watch the office. Everyone else is home."

"Because of what's going on?" I asked.

Erin nodded. "You'd think there'd be more of a need, but students are busy studying and I think most people are unwilling to look at the deeper meaning of what's happening."

I looked behind me. There was a long black sofa of some sort of faux-leather that might have been popular in 1980. The wood desk behind which Erin sat was large and heavy and probably of the same era if the scratches were any indication. The woodwork on the walls, which came about halfway up had been painted white and the upper walls, plain drywall there, had been painted a pastel blue so light if it hadn't been next to true white I'd never have noticed the blue.

A large framed photo of the campus as it had been fifty years ago hung on the wall. I paused to take that in.

The bungalow was there along with my dorm and one of the guys' dorms. A different building sat near where the cafeteria was, more like a house. The old library building was there, too, all ivy-covered and sat in shadows of trees that towered over it. None of the buildings matched.

"It was a lot smaller back then," Erin said, walking over behind me. She settled on the sofa and looked at me.

I sat on the far end, sort of trying to face her, though it made me uncomfortable to have my back to the door, where shadows might linger and attack even in the daylight. I rubbed the back of my neck to calm the imaginary sensations of something cold and hard about to grab me and perhaps tear out my throat.

"A woman in my dorm was injured the other night," I said. "I was with her and I felt something there. I thought I saw something that doesn't exist. And my roommate has left because her mom is certain this has to do with the church burning down and our school not crowning a Lucia Bride."

Erin nodded at me, thoughtfully. I might have been bringing a problem about schoolwork or home life to her. She took me seriously and not like someone who was having a breakdown.

"Lucia Bride has always been slightly more pagan than Christian. She's a martyr like all the saints, but, for some reason, we still honor her in ways we don't honor other saints in our church. The Catholic Church honors many of the saints, but not Lutherans. Even so, St. Lucia remains venerated in our church." Erin went silent for a moment, thinking. "I don't believe what is happening is because we didn't crown a Lucia Bride. There was a girl awarded the scholarship, so technically we *do* have a Lucia Bride."

"I went to the church—not inside or anything. I walked around the back and I saw this guy. I thought he was the pastor there, but I guess…" I trailed off, waiting to see if Erin had heard.

"The pastor died in the basement." Erin finished and sighed. "The person you saw could have been anyone. Worse, he could have been the person who is hurting people. I hope you won't go out there again, even in daylight. Stay where people can see you, where people are around."

"Parents are calling and saying that there's more crime and deaths all over the place." I waited to see how Erin would respond.

"I've heard people seem to be noticing more crime as if whatever is going on is widespread. I don't know why, nor do I understand the timing. I teach the words of the gospel and those can protect you. If you believe that Jesus saved you and that he protects you, then I believe you are protected against anything that isn't fully human. The human dangers, those He expects you to be proactive about, though He wouldn't want us to live in fear. Just don't go wandering around in deserted areas when you know people are dying." Erin gave me a nod to punctuate her comments.

I appreciated that she was keeping the religious aspect minimal. Maybe she was doing it on purpose so that I wouldn't equate religion with whatever was out there in the darkness.

"The man at the church told me that I had to find the answers inside, but not inside the church," I said, finally. "I keep wondering what inside he was talking about."

Erin frowned. She said nothing for a few minutes, thinking. "When I use terminology like that, I might be talking about inside yourself. In your head or your heart. What you know already."

No sudden lightbulb came on. I think I had considered that when I'd been thinking about the imagination. I didn't know if that was the proper response or not.

"You're very courageous to come here and talk about this," Erin said. "Most students are keeping their heads down and avoiding the subject. I know you're all trying to study. You, however, are here asking questions. I think it's very hard to admit when we've seen something that makes no sense, that we believe is something we couldn't have seen."

I hadn't exactly told her everything I'd seen. I wasn't interested in that. However, I was annoyed that she had only a few platitudes to give me.

I stood up, pulling up my backpack. I glanced once more at the old image of the school. The old library building seemed to beckon me. I knew I'd be making a stop on my way back to the dorm.

Chapter Nineteen

Behind clouds that seemed a mile thick, the sun hid, slipping lower in the sky each minute. I wouldn't have much time to explore the old library building before dark. I hurried across the silent campus, passing only one other woman who scurried past me towards the cafeteria, perhaps to beg some afternoon or evening food.

Or maybe she was a lucky person rich enough to afford the hotel instead of the less secure dorms and she'd just finished a final and was racing back to lock herself in before full dark fell.

I paused outside the old library building, noting the fog that hung around the base. The once red bricks had turned black in some areas. White mortar patches made the building a patchwork that was actually quite pleasing to the eye.

Three stories high, it sat off-center. Two large cedars sat to the left of the building, offering shade and giving it proportion. Now, of course, it housed the math depart-ment. The first floor had been completely redone in bright white drywall and new electrical fixtures that kept shadows at bay and housed most of the offices. Up the old staircase, the second and third floors weren't as nicely redone but there was a thoroughly modern elevator sitting next to the stairs for those who couldn't use the stairwell. The main staircase, I was told during orientation, was still original to the building.

Lights glowed from the windows, though I saw no one in the building, the staff who worked there perhaps given leave to work from home as much as possible. The professors, of course, would have to come in to administer their finals, but the secretary and any assistants wouldn't be needed.

I turned, biting my lip. What might be in the old library? The answers were inside. I had a feeling they weren't really inside me. Why the library building? The fog around me gathered in ever larger clouds of pale gray. One floated towards me, wafting over me, leaving me as cold and damp as if I'd walked through a ghost.

Not that I really know what walking through a ghost felt like, but the fog felt as I imagined it would with the slight scent of rot, and the chill cold that ate away at my body heat despite my heavy coat. I shivered and put my hands in my pockets and walked a bit faster along the cobbled walk. Though the clouds threatened, they'd dropped no new snow on the ground and the walks were mostly clear.

If it had snowed again, no doubt the school would have had to call in the groundskeepers to clear the paths as they always did, often before the sun was up, so that walkways would be safe for students by the time classes rolled around. No doubt it would be a difficult choice for whoever had to make the call. Potentially endanger workers from something no one understood or put students at risk of a fall and injury.

I reached my dorm without further incident. Still shivering, I slipped inside. The desk worker's head snapped up as if she thought I might be a monster breaking in. The tension in her shoulders told me she wasn't happy about having to be on shift.

"You okay?" I asked.

"Fine," she said, turning away, clearly not willing to discuss it. I waited a bit, but she didn't even turn to look at me.

I headed up the stairs. I'd look up information on the old library when I got to my room. For now, I had only two more nights and one more final to worry about. Then I could head home. Hopefully.

Old buildings house the strangest acoustics and I heard murmurs and whispers from the rooms on the other floors. It wasn't uncommon. It mostly happened at night and until I had heard the legends about our ghost, I thought that the sounds were the reason the dorm was thought to be haunted. They probably still played a large role in the ongoing legends as no one I knew of had seen the ghost.

The wing doors were all closed. I decided to turn the opposite direction, walking across the upstairs lounge to the other wing's door and check out their haunted kitchen. While it held a different configuration of a long back wall of cabinets, refrigerator, and microwave with a tiny table with two chairs facing each other against the wall by the door, like ours it smelled most profoundly of popcorn. A hundred years from now I had a feeling the dorm kitchens would smell like popcorn no matter that many students now brought their own microwaves or popcorn poppers to school with them. The window at the far end, which ours didn't have, had a blind that was closed.

These cabinets were oak stained and had darkened with age, making them look blackened in places almost as if someone had started a fire. That wasn't impossible, but I'm sure that would have been added to the ghost stories. The room felt colder than the rest of the dorm. While that may or may not have had anything to do with the ghost, I had no doubt that it fed the legends.

After closing the door carefully lest someone be listening for the ghost, I settled into the chair facing the door. The light was on in the kitchen. It had been when I got there and I didn't change that. While ghosts were supposed to prefer the dark, I had no desire to sit in the dark waiting. Other creatures, less potentially friendly creatures might find their way to me in the darkness.

I pulled out my laptop and started a search on the old library building at HLC. It wasn't as easy as I'd hoped. In movies and on television the hero always finds exactly what they're looking for without going through a hundred different searches that dead end. It's always tidily done with no time wasted. Either they knew things I didn't or stories played that way because of the dullness of watching someone look things up on their computer.

I did learn that the original library building had been built back in 1903 upon the university's founding. It had served as the entire campus, and had a single dorm that looked similar in size right next to it. The black and white photograph showed the cedars nearby as being much smaller then, or perhaps they weren't even the same trees.

The oldest of the guy's dorms, Birger, was built in 1919. In 1940, my dorm, Piehl, was built. Two years later the two original buildings were joined by an addition. Several smaller buildings that had once been homes near the university were purchased and used for offices.

I would have liked a floor plan of the old library. If I

were going to search for some oddity, that would certainly be a help. But not such floorplan existed online, not that I could find. There wasn't even a whole lot about the wonderful people who had founded HLC, only that they had been devoted churchgoers who wanted education for their families without having to send them far away from home.

I leaned back and stretched my neck. The room seemed darker than when I'd started reading. While dusk had likely arrived and it was darker outside, the blind on the window kept out the daylight so it didn't seem logical that the room would be darker. I felt my shoulders tense in anxiety. I sniffed.

I smelled a hint of lavender. My aunt had an antique dresser that had belonged to her grandmother and although Aunt Nicky wasn't fond of sachets, her grandmother had been. When you opened the drawers you always smelled traces of lavender.

I breathed in and out. Maybe there was a ghost and maybe she could tell me something. I hoped that since I was putting myself in a position to see a ghost, she'd come through on the information part of things.

My tense muscles began to ache, but I waited. And waited. I jumped when the plumbing burped as it does all over the building now and again.

Someone giggled. Either the girls were really loud or someone was in the room.

"Hello?" I whispered. My voice scratched against my throat, hoarse with tension. It was a good thing I was trying to be quiet because I couldn't have yelled if my life depended upon it. For a moment I reflected that perhaps that's the way the pizza delivery woman had felt.

A shadow moved from the door and seemed to settle in the chair across from me.

"They're here again, aren't they?"

I knew someone or something had spoken but the words came to me oddly. If I had been recording this, it was the sort of sound that a recorder wouldn't pick up because the voice might have been all in my head. Or not.

I nodded. I didn't want to speak out loud lest someone hear me and come in and see me talking to an empty chair.

"I didn't kill myself. They say that. They say it was over a boy who didn't return my love. They're wrong."

"I believe you." I had to say that aloud. There wasn't a way to convey my belief in a nod or a shake of my head. I suppose I could have written something. Still, I kept my voice low. I hoped the girls that had the rooms nearest this one weren't listening.

"They came then, too. Then the church was built to contain them. I didn't think they'd come back." The shadow moved ever so slightly. Shadow might not have been a very accurate description. It was gray, certainly, but there was something much more three dimensional about it than there was with the average shadow. And, it was lighter than the other shadows that gathered in the corners of the kitchen.

"The church burned," I said. "The pastor was inside."

A light breeze ruffled the hair around my ears. I felt something cold near my ear. It disappeared as fast as it appeared.

"They're back, then."

"Some people say it's about Lucia Bride." I figured why not toss that out there. Maybe I'd learn something.

"St. Lucia was powerful and because she was a patron of keeping the darkness at bay this time of year, cele-brating her, the belief in her, kept the darkness from overwhelming the world. Without her, it's easier for them to cross into the world of light and love."

"No one believes anything any longer."

"I thought that, too. But there are always believers."

"Things have happened in places hundreds and thousands of miles from here," I said. I needed the ghost to understand how big this was.

"Then it has gotten worse since my day."

"Did they push you?" I asked.

"I sacrificed myself for the light."

My stomach sank. I had no desire to go leaping out a window to sacrifice myself to save the dorm.

"It helped, but not because I died."

Some relief flooded through me. I wondered if I could pretend to fly out the window and save my life.

"It helped because I was brave enough to offer myself for others. I would lead them back to the light with the strength of my belief. That's what Lucia stood for. It's why she is the barrier between the creatures of the dark and the beings of this world. We are not always good or strong or loving. But we have that power."

Relief flooded through me for an instant. I didn't have to die. However, someone needed to offer themselves, somehow, and lead others to save the world from the darkness."

"There is help if you need it." My ghost sounded almost shy.

"Where?" I asked.

"They'll come to you as they're needed. You have to trust. Have faith."

The shadow slipped away. A light grayness slid beneath the door and was gone. The corners of the kitchen no longer seemed so dark. The smell of lavender disappeared completely and the normal scent of popcorn returned.

Something thumped out in the hallway. I waited behind the door to the kitchen, hoping whatever was out would not choose to come inside. I wished I hadn't come to the kitchen and had instead locked myself in my own room. Now I might be trapped inside a room without a lock on the door while a creature roamed the hallways of the fourth floor.

I held my breath listening to whatever was on the other side of the door. I had been in the process of standing up and now I squatted near the chair, not daring to settle on it in case the wood creaked or groaned. The thumping moved off and I stood, leaning back against the counter, watching the door, waiting for the knob to turn before it would open and I'd see the monster I'd been dreading.

A door slammed and there was silence. I heard a few gasps from the rooms around me. The bathroom door opened with a slight creak. I waited but heard nothing but the sounds of someone running down the hallway.

The door that had opened had been the door to the stairwell at the end. I opened the kitchen door and peeked out. The hall was dimly lit. Only the emergency lights were on. It wasn't late enough for the lights to be down even if the dorm hadn't been leaving on all the lights. I hurried towards the end of the hall.

I looked through the window in the upper part of the door before flinging it open to go into the lounge. I saw nothing.

"Hurry." The disembodied voice whispered to me.

So far she hadn't led me wrong even if she hadn't helped me. I opened the door and fled across the lounge to my own wing. I ran down the silent hall which hung heavy with shadows. The emergency lights flickered and buzzed more loudly than I'd ever heard them.

I felt around in my pocket for the key to my dorm room. For a moment all I felt was the cloth of my pants and my stomach twisted in knots as I pictured it lying on the floor in the kitchen. The image was so real for just a moment that I almost fled to the kitchen, hoping to find a way to bar the door against a monster even though I knew my keys hadn't fallen out of my pocket back there.

Finally, my fingers touched cool metal and I pulled the key out and slammed it into the lock. Weeks of practice of not looking at the knob when I inserted the key, of trying to be quiet when Jen might already be asleep guided my hand. I opened my door just as the door to the lounge opened.

The thing behind the lounge door was larger than the opening. Cartoonists drew heads smaller than the one on this thing. Sharp tusks rose from the jaw and curved inward almost hitting the eyes which glowed pinkish gold in the dim lighting. It blinked twice as I pushed open my door.

The slight squeak of a floorboard echoed in the hall as I stepped over the threshold. The creature raised the monstrously huge skull and glared at me, its skin greenish-brown and pockmarked. The body was humanoid but humped over like an ape rather than standing tall like a man. It used an enormous fist, perhaps the hand that I'd seen the other night, to help it walk.

I slammed the door closed, flipping the lock before I drew another breath, the image of the creature heading towards me in the hallway burned into my mind. I leaned my back against the wood of the door, looking around for something, *anything*, to help me hold it closed even as the thumps of the creature drew closer.

The doors were newer than the rest of the building, the wood, perhaps, stronger. Or maybe the hollow core doors were flimsier than the walls around me. The microwave cart might fit down the entry hall to help block the door but it had wheels and wouldn't hold. The loveseat needed to angled just so and I couldn't lift it alone to make it fit. And even that could be pushed away easily.

If the creature could break through the door I was dead.

It pounded on the door. I felt the wood pulse beneath its fists, though it held, for now. My heart raced. My hands were sweating. I heard whimpering from somewhere and I wondered if Jen had come back.

I saw no one in the room I had left well lit, blinds drawn over the desks. Something else tapped at the window. I slid down to a sitting position and wrapped my arms around my knees. If only someone would make a sound somewhere else.

I heard a scream outside. Another girl. My head raised. The sound stopped, suddenly cut off.

The thing outside my door thumped its way down the hall. The creature at the glass continued to tap and bang on it. Then it began to scratch, making a sound that sent chills up my spine and made my stomach feel as if it were going to revolt. This was a thousand times worse than scratching nails across a chalkboard.

Finally, that too stopped. No slowing, just a toddler losing interest in a toy. I breathed out. I started to shake. Only then did I realize that my clothing was soaked through.

I stood up quietly, looking around as if something could have come through the door and I would have missed it. I wanted to laugh at that image but I bit it back. I had no desire to draw attention to my room again. Bad enough that the creature, the monster, was out there.

I pulled off my soaked clothing and changed into sweats. I even put my boots back on, though where I might be going I had no idea. I draped my coat across the top of the dresser. Then I went to the window and pulled the blind aside just a hair so I could peer out.

I half expected huge eyes to meet mine on the other side of the glass but nothing was there. I could see nothing outside the window but dark gray. Fog obscured everything. I thought I saw lights to guide the poor souls who might have had to go out. I thought of will-of-the-wisps leading people to their doom in the marshes. No marshes there on the cliffs of the Northshore, but that didn't mean the unwary couldn't be led astray. I'd mention it in the morning. If I saw anyone.

The ghost had said someone needed to lead, like St. Lucia. To offer themselves. She made it sound like she'd jumped thinking that was leading but had said that was wrong. Was death off the table or not? I bit my lip, hesitating.

Belief wasn't off the table, unfortunately. While I'd grown up in a church-going household, I'm not sure I had belief, not like that. I appreciated the Lutheran campuses. Not only were the hymns and sermons comfortably familiar, they didn't require that I go to church or that I discuss everything I believed. No doubt it was the Northern European influence. Hadn't I heard jokes that a Lutheran missionary was an oxymoron?

Did I have faith? I went to church now and then. I didn't question it, exactly. I wasn't devout, certainly. I'd spent my life rebelling against the life my parents lived. I didn't exactly want to settle in La Crosse and do property management. I just didn't know what I did want to do. If I had something to head towards maybe my rebellion would have been more effective than the escapist use of drugs I'd done before.

Teaching business law would be fun. Working in business law would be even better, but I have to admit, I wasn't certain I could take the kind of pressure that went on in law school. Still, I found that interesting. I could be a paralegal, maybe.

My career goals were nothing to the creatures out and about. My faith was. My ability to offer myself and lead. The biggest hurdle was that I didn't want to die. No matter what awaited me on the other side, so to speak, I had no desire to give up this life. I hadn't even begun to live my life. I'd been busy avoiding living the life my parents wanted for me.

So now, if not me, then someone, had to offer themselves to the monsters and lead us all in faith. If I couldn't do it, who else could? Maybe the campus minister I'd talked to earlier today would be willing. I mean, wasn't that her job? To lead people in faith?

I started getting really annoyed with her. It seemed like the kind of thing that religious leaders should know. Like, I knew there were books on how to lead a parish and all because I'd picked up a lot from pre-seminary students at my various Lutheran educational institutions. This meant that someone should have written down what to do if creatures of the dark appeared around the solstice and started murdering a few people and terrorizing others.

It should also have pointed out that a person of faith would have to take the lead.

That wasn't my job.

Something banged on my door again. I was too angry to be scared. I considered opening it and screaming into the large monster's face. Instead, I stood silently near the desk, looking at the door. The knob turned back and forth and then the thing moved on.

I heard it slam its huge meaty fists into the door across the way. Screams reached my ears.

It paused there to bang on the door. More screams and tears, loud enough that I heard them through the walls and the hallway. My neighbors were terrified.

No RA ran down the hall to help. I didn't hear any phones being picked up, voices calling for campus security. I might have been the only person around who could do something. Like I had when I'd heard the scream from outside, I stood there. Because I am not a leader and certainly not one of the faithful.

I slumped down on my bed and pulled a pillow over my head to try and drown out the sounds of terror that continued to reach me.

Chapter Twenty-One

The screams calmed or, at least, I couldn't hear them through the pillow. For all I knew Cassidy and Kennedy had just screamed away their voices. The creature continued to thump on their door.

"Let it go away," I murmured, not sure who I was talking to. Maybe it was a prayer. It occurred to me that praying like this wasn't about faith. It was wishful thinking. I was wishing the creature to leave though I had no real expectation that it would.

Then it moved on to my next-door neighbors. No one screamed from there. I knew Dee and Wendy were home. They had a wheel on their door that said things like "Up for visitors," "Invitation only," "Studying," and the like. And yes, there was a space that said, "Date". Wendy had more dates than Dee, so far as I could tell. I hadn't noticed the wheel when I'd hurried by their door but I usually noticed when it wasn't up on the visitor's section because it was almost always there.

The thumping didn't go on too long. It moved down

the hallway. I heard a gasp. The thumping went on longer there before the creature moved on.

There was no way to know if this was the same thing that had chased me or if it was a different creature. It sounded large like the thing that I'd seen in the hallway.

Suddenly, I remembered the poor woman down at the front desk. I hoped she'd gotten away and hidden before the thing or things came in. There was an office behind the desk. It certainly wasn't optimal but at least, like the kitchen, it was a place to hide. I shuddered thinking of her terror.

Someone needed to do something. I remembered my conversation with the ghost. Perhaps that someone needed to be me. No one else was tossing out ideas.

I pulled out my phone. If there were ideas, no one was messaging me. I looked up the email list for the wing. Nothing.

I sent a quick message to the list, hoping someone would answer. "*Is everyone in their rooms?*" I typed.

Almost immediately, I got two responses. Cassidy said she and Kennedy were. Naomi wrote back as well. It was followed by Rebecca's note to say she was in her room. She also gave orders for all of us to stay in our rooms. Like anyone was going to go walking out into the hallway with that thing out running around out there.

"*Anyone know about the front desk person?*" I wrote.

Nothing came back. I hit refresh several times, hoping something would come in. A couple of other people checked in for themselves and their roommates. It looked like most of our wing was safe in their rooms.

Marble wrote, "*I hope she's okay.*"

"*Door should be locked,*" Rebecca wrote, which wasn't really an answer to the front desk person. It was barely six. It almost sounded like she was going to be mad that the front desk person didn't walk out into the lobby, amidst all these creatures, and locked the front door or something. Although the door was being locked earlier than usual, I hadn't heard that the front desk was closing sooner than usual.

At least Marble appeared to care.

"Hannah hasn't gotten back from her final," MacKenzie wrote.

"If you have her number, tell her not to leave alone," I sent back almost immediately.

A few other people did oh nos.

"She texted me about half an hour ago that she had called Campus Security to bring her back," MacKenzie replied.

I didn't like that. No one said anything. Not even Rebecca, who was starting to piss me off. An RA was supposed to lead. I couldn't say she had to have faith because that's never been a must have here, but she was the person we had to go to if we had a problem. She ought to be problem-solving. Instead, she hadn't even done a check-in.

I lay back on the bed, looking at my phone. I could just as easily be using my laptop but I'd have to move to get that out of my bag. I longed for someone I could count on to send out an email to ask if we were okay. Normally, a warm and fuzzy type as an RA would have irritated me, but tonight that's exactly what I wanted.

I read through the notes that came through. The rest of the wing was there. Only Hannah was missing from our little section of the building. I didn't have a way to contact everyone else in the dorm. Jen checked in from her hotel room with her mom. They were safe. They'd eaten a large late lunch and were going to snack on cheese and crackers when they got hungry. They'd be leaving after Jen's final tomorrow.

I wanted someone to step up. Surely, the school couldn't expect a student to be the one leading people through this nightmare. Surely, the *world* couldn't expect it.

The world, though, probably didn't really know what was happening. A few sets of parents from this school and perhaps a few others knew. The parents were adults in a way I was not.

Someone knocked on the door. A normal knock. Like a human.

I sat up.

"Who's there?" I asked.

No answer. Still, I stood up and walked over to the door. I lay down on the floor to look under the crack of the door.

Light came through. Two heavy feet waited, clad in dark boots. Heavy boots. The huge creature was learning.

It knocked again. Still, the light touch as if a human were outside the door. I waited, not responding, looking at the feet. I'd left my phone on the bed. I pushed myself up to let the others know that the creature had learned to knock.

I picked up my phone when I heard it move down the hallway. I started typing as quickly as I could, hoping it would be fast enough.

I didn't hear the knock on the next door. I was too far away and too intent upon the message. I did, however, hear the tell-tale squeak of a door opening a crack. For an instant, I was shocked that anyone would be foolish enough to peek out considering what was out there. Then I realized that the other women on my wing hadn't seen the thing I'd seen. At best they'd seen shadows and maybe a face.

Someone screamed. I dropped my phone and ran to the door.

Chapter Twenty-Two

I stopped to think in front of the closed door rather than running out into the hallway. Another scream.

I couldn't not peek out.

Stupid girls in horror movies always run towards the monster to try and save a friend. If I got out of this, I wasn't going to laugh about their idiocy any longer.

I unlocked the door and pulled, just a crack in case the screams were a decoy.

The sound was louder. Nothing waited at my door, ready to push inside.

Outside, next door, a large shadow moved in the doorway of my neighbors. I had nothing with which to battle it. I'd be dead. I closed the door softly and took note of what I had in my room. Faith. Yeah right.

I looked in the little case where I kept jewelry, mostly cheap trinkets I'd picked up. I was not the sort of girl who wore a cross. Jen often did, but she'd packed the little box in which she kept the necklace with the cross.

A Bible sat on Jen's bookshelves, one for a class she'd taken. It wasn't beautiful but it was the word.

Faith was about something I believed in. Ultimately, though the book was heavy, I didn't think it would do more than pound the creature upside the head. I didn't have much hope that it would make any difference.

This was not what I needed. Unfortunately, I didn't know what I believed in. I couldn't count on goodness. I certainly didn't believe that anyone would come and help me. Although the ghost had told me that helpers would show up when needed.

"What do I have?" I cried. Thumps came from next door. Hard thumps and groans. Someone was still screaming. All this had taken only a moment though I felt as if it had taken half a lifetime.

I smelled lavender. "Take your phone," the ghost said. She was still a shadow but I thought I saw a hint of a dress with a full skirt that ended just below her knees.

I grabbed the phone. I did believe in technology. Maybe that would be enough.

Heart thudding in terror, I grasped the phone with palms that were already slick with sweat. The phone threatened to go flying from my grip.

I held it close to my chest, not at all certain what it was I should do.

I opened the door.

The lavender scent was overpowered by something dank and moldy, like an old book that had gotten wet. I stepped out into the hallway.

"Stop it!" I screamed.

Like yelling was going to do anything.

The sounds from the other room quieted. Something heavy moved across the floor. The shadow creature looked out. Something red dripped from its fingers in the dim light.

The ghost rushed at it.

The creature drew back, probably startled more than terrified.

When the ghost passed through it, it looked at me again, its eyes almond-shaped and glowing.

It opened its mouth slightly, tiny sharp pointed teeth between the two tusks. A greenish-gray tongue slithered out, too thin and narrow compared to the rest of the creature. I shuddered.

It took a step out the door so that it stood facing me. I held up the phone. Like that was going to help. I had a fricken phone against a creature with a head that nearly rubbed the ceiling even when it leaned over like an ape. Stupid horror movie girls my ass. I was dumber than anyone I'd seen on the television.

"Get back," the ghost whispered. She stood so close to me the scent of lavender smelled too strongly in my nose. I tasted it in the back of my throat and between that and my terror, my breath refused to come.

I stepped back. Just one step. Into the room.

My hands shook.

The creature walked closer to my room. The windowless kitchen was between my room and the one next door. It wasn't actually next door because it was between what I thought of as Jen's sleeping cubby and the hall.

I backed into my room.

Either Dee or Wendy slammed their door. The creature looked back at it.

Then it turned to me, a new fire in its eyes. Before it had had several people to attack. Now it had only me.

I slammed my door and turned the lock just in time to hear it begin to bang on my door, once more.

I expected the door to hold like it had last time. Either the wood was weaker because of the previous assault or the creature was angrier than it had been last time. A crack appeared in the center of the door. It was going to get through.

Still nothing in my room to use as a weapon. My backpack held a few books, my metal water bottle, and my laptop. I hadn't had a chance to unpack it. It was heavy, so maybe I could throw that.

I heard the sound of splintering wood. I grabbed the pack, dismayed that it suddenly didn't feel heavy at all.

The creature looked through the hole in the door though it was much too small for it to crawl through. I had a flashback to the classic scene in the movie *The Shining*. Except this thing didn't even have an evil sense of humor to lessen the tension of the moment.

My hands shook. My heart threatened to beat its way out of my chest and go fleeing through the window leaving the rest of my body behind. My mouth was so dry that even if I could remember how to scream, I doubted I could make a sound.

The creature punched through more wood. I couldn't hear a thing over the drumming of my heart. If only my heart really would run off, then I'd be dead and not have to go through the last few moments of my life with this monster, moments that were going to be painful and frightening.

The moldy book smell hit me harder.

The creature pushed its way through the hole, now so much bigger. The sound of wood breaking came to me from an impossible distance though I stood only a few feet away, holding my backpack.

"Take that!" someone yelled. Also far away. Kennedy maybe. I didn't hear her yell often. She wasn't a yeller. But it could be her.

The creature turned. I saw something smoking on its back as if it had been wounded.

Kennedy did something else. The creature started to stand wrong like it was going to lie down. I watched as the feet began to melt into the floor, a dark black shadow.

With nothing to hold it up, the heavy body began to slither into shadow and slowly dissipate. It became smaller and smaller until Kennedy was visible from behind, two large open water bottles in her hands, a shocked look on her face.

"I didn't…." she started and stopped, her voice now her usual lower octave.

The head of the creature snarled, a sound like a dog about to attack.

Cassidy came out and dumped the water from her water bottle over the thing's head. Smoke came out of the hair and it began to melt into the floor, rather like Dorothy's experience with the Wicked Witch of the West.

"What the hell?" I muttered, going to the door to look out. Not hard. I didn't exactly have a door, just a wood frame inside the door frame.

"I didn't know what else to do to distract it. I poured water on it," Kennedy said. "It worked?"

Of course it worked. She'd watched *The Wizard of Oz* a million times, collected the books, studied it. She'd done her term paper on the story. Water destroyed the evil witch. Her belief had destroyed the monster. Having seen water destroying the thing, Cassidy believed.

And now so did I.

Chapter Twenty-Three

I heard something on the stairs next to my room.

"Kitchen," I ordered and hurried inside. I still held my backpack, with my water bottle. As Cassidy and Kennedy hurried inside, catching on to what I wanted them to do, I pulled out my own metal water bottle, not nearly as big as Kennedy's but hopefully large enough to slow something down.

A smaller shadow pushed through the door to the stairs. That door was considered a fire door and those were some of the heaviest doors. Even so, the little thing pushed it like it wasn't a problem. It looked like a cross between a toddler and a squirrel with a longer snout on a human-like face and brownish fur covering much of its back. It walked upright but had a tail, though not as bushy as that of a squirrel. It grinned at me with a mouth full of sharp little teeth.

It moved as fast as a squirrel and I barely had the bottle open to begin pouring water on it before it launched itself to my shoulder. I felt the weight of it, heavier than I would have expected. Sharp nails dug into my flesh just below my shoulder.

The water in the bottle was cold from being outside, despite the insulation of the cup. Without that insulation, I'd probably have had ice.

The creature squealed, a sound more like that of a small animal than a human child. For that I was grateful.

It, too, began to melt away, leaving only a surprisingly large, thick black claw stuck in my sweater. I pulled it out and looked at it in the light from the kitchen.

"It looks sharp," Cassidy said.

"It was," I said, looking down at the spot of blood on my shirt.

I heard more of the creatures running up the stairs. Kennedy had filled every pan she could with water. She was now filling all the mismatched mugs and glasses in the cupboard with water as well. I set my open water bottle down and grabbed a pan.

Four of the small creatures scampered through the door. They didn't pause to let me get my bearings. They just flew at me, almost as if they knew where I was before they even entered the hallway. I threw the water at them. Fortunately, the pan was fairly large and I got at least some water on each of them or I'd have been injured.

The only reason I wouldn't have been killed or injured despite hitting each of them at least a little was because Cassidy was right there and tossed another pan of water on them.

Bringing our weapons back, we refilled. Nothing thumped on the stairs.

I went to Dee and Wendy's and asked if they were okay.

"She's bleeding, still," Wendy said. "It's bad."

"Call 911," I said.

"She doesn't want someone else to get hurt," Wendy said as I heard a low groan from Dee.

"Make sure you have water. If something tries to get at you, water will destroy it. Kennedy and Cassidy and I have it out here."

"Water?" Marble said. Her room was the next down.

"Water," I said. "We're in the kitchen. Maybe see if there's more stuff to gather up to hold water in the bathroom."

Marble opened her door slowly, peering out, making sure this wasn't a joke. She hurried across the way. The bright bathroom lights spilled out into the dim hallway. I grabbed my newly refilled water bottle and hurried down to the end of the hall to turn on the regular lights. The power wasn't out because we had lights in the room. Someone or something had turned off the hall lights.

The hall immediately brightened. I breathed a sigh of relief just as the door behind me slammed open. I jumped.

I turned. It was another of the large creatures, followed by something vaguely dog-like, if dogs were related to bears. It had long dark fur and a snout full of teeth, the double-layered teeth of movie nightmares. I tossed my water at both of them and ran back to the kitchen, yelling for Cassidy to bring out a huge pan of water.

Cassidy came out and tossed water at the creatures, splashing me in the face with it. The liquid was cold and I shuddered. The creatures behind me roared and screamed in pain.

After my brief pause to get my bearings, I hurried back into the kitchen bringing out another pan, to toss water on the creatures before they came any further.

Cassidy was right with me, carrying a large mixing bowl and tossing water at them.

Marble came out of the bath and tossed a bucket of water over their heads.

As they melted away into the now soaked wood floors, her eyes widened. "It works!" she screamed.

Lori came out and hurried into the bathroom, perhaps to fill another container with water.

Naomi and her roommate, Sandi, opened their door and joined us in the water brigade.

Slowly, the rest of our wing brought out their water bottles, some popcorn bowls, and even a few travel mugs and filled them up with water.

"Find flashlights," I told everyone. The creatures had hated light. They probably still hated light and had learned to turn lights off. Still, they had to turn off the flashlights first before they could get to us. It might not be enough but it might buy someone some time.

Only four girls left. The rest of us clearly relied on our phones for light. I didn't want everyone running down phone batteries in case we had an emergency. Most of the flashlights were little penlights carried on keychains. Naomi checked in the bathroom and found one of those blocky construction style flashlights which she carried out.

"We should go clear the rest of the dorm," I said.

Several others nodded.

"We should leave a couple of people here to make sure that Wendy and Dee remain safe," someone said. "Keep one of the buckets here."

We had found a regular cleaning bucket and then one of those industrial mop bucket things in metal. It was heavy as heck. Someone had the brilliant idea to set it right in front of a door in case the creatures tried to come through.

We got volunteers to man the nearly deserted wing. They'd stay in the kitchen so they had access to water. The bathroom door swung open and closed but didn't rely on a latch. The kitchen door, at least, had that. If it came to that, it would be easier for them to barricade themselves in the kitchen than the bathroom. They got two of the penlights, just in case. We were going to need the brighter construction-sized flashlight.

"I'm thinking we start on the fifth floor and work our way down. That way if there's something upstairs, it can't come down behind us," I said.

Kennedy nodded quickly. Naomi followed and so did the others.

I moved the big bucket with the mop and nodded at one of the women who would stay behind to let her know it could be returned as soon as we were all in the stairwell. I pushed open the door to the fire stairs. It was more protected there than in the lounge. Nothing jumped out at me.

"There might be creatures coming from behind. I want someone with the light back there and someone with a good-sized container," I said. I had a saucepan filled halfway up with water. It seemed the most expedient that way. I wouldn't be spilling everything, but it still had enough to give a good splash. I thought it would probably completely take out one of the smaller creatures and buy enough time against the larger monster until someone else threw water on it.

I climbed the first flight of stairs, going slowly, looking up. I heard nothing, but that meant nothing. Around the next corner, I looked up at the door. While the door was in shadow, the darkness looked like normal shadows. I hurried up. Nothing attacked. I flicked on the landing light, brightening the space.

Nothing waited in a corner.

I opened the door to the hallway slowly.

Immediately, two of the small creatures and a dog-like thing attacked. The small creatures chittered as they ran at me. The dog-like thing moved as silently as the shadow it resembled when I opened the door.

I tossed the water and pulled back so that the door closed.

I let Kennedy go next. She held the cleaning bucket which had more water. She waited for a few seconds before pushing the door open and then only a crack. Nothing came at us. I stretched to look over her shoulder.

Part of the doglike creature had already melted. The tail still whipped, the end holding something like a scorpion stinger. Kennedy threw water on that.

We all proceeded down the hall to the kitchen. Kennedy and I filled our containers. Cassidy came in and started pulling out other containers. The saucepans might be smaller but they were easier to carry than the mixing bowls.

"Leave the mixing bowls for people to guard the wing," I said. "They won't have to carry them so far."

"Good idea." Cassidy pulled out all the other containers. My wingmates traded in their less useful items for better. Naomi had already started down the hall to find another bucket.

Someone else had flipped on the main hall lights. I heard a thump at the far end. Naomi ducked into the bathroom as the far door opened.

All of us hurried towards the shadowy creature that came through. This was different from the large creatures that we had fought on our floor. It was less solid, more like a creature of shadow than of substance. More ghostly, I guess. Still, it smelled of mold and slightly of sulfur.

I hit it with the water in the pan. It dissolved easily leaving only a wet spot on the floor.

Someone cheered.

"It's okay!" I called to the fifth-floor wing. "Water kills them. We're clearing the dorm if you want to come out and help."

"Who are you?" a woman called.

Another woman, perhaps braver, perhaps more foolish, poked her head out her room. "It's the fourth-floor girls. I recognize Marble."

Other doors opened.

Discussion started. Their RA came out, frowning. "Where's Rebecca?" she asked.

"Rebecca didn't want to join us," I said. Several of us had asked her. Naomi had even emailed her on the list in case Rebecca thought the monsters were playing with her. She said we were being ridiculous and would get ourselves killed.

The RA looked skeptical. Just then one of the little skittering creatures came through the fire door. Someone, I didn't see who, tossed their water on it. It screeched and started to melt.

"That's so wild," the RA said.

She started organizing her wing. One of the women on the wing had twisted an ankle in the snow so couldn't move that fast. She and her roommate would stay on the wing. We fixed up the mop bucket near the fire door like we had on our wing. The weight would make it harder to open. Then the creatures would have to hope they didn't spill any of the water if they did get through.

"What made you try water?" the RA asked. As we got closer to her room, I noted her name was Sonja. She looked like a Sonja with pale blonde hair in a braid that fell past her mid-back.

"I panicked," Kennedy said. "I love *The Wizard of Oz*

and all I had was water. It killed the witch so I tossed it at the creature. Mina would have died otherwise."

"It worked. So we all started using it," I said. I wasn't going to talk about belief. Then everyone would doubt their belief was strong enough and we'd be back at square one.

"They're out in the snow, though," Kelly said, frowning.

I shrugged. "Maybe there's more minerals or lead or something in this water. The building is really old."

Kelly nodded. "Or they need liquid and the snow is frozen. Maybe it has something to do with that."

Whatever worked for her.

I headed towards the door to the lounge on the fifth floor.

"We should station someone at the lounge stairs," I said. "They can race to the kitchen if they need to. Someone with a bucket, in case something comes up. This floor will be the most dangerous right now because we've cleared the fewest places."

"Leave two," Sonja said. "Brittney would be one of my picks."

Brittany had a long heavy flashlight of the sort that the police carried. Her father was in law enforcement and he wanted her protected in case she walked around campus on her own. She wasn't a large girl, but she walked with a confidence that came from years of doing martial arts. I'd seen her practicing in the main lounge from time to time.

"I'll stay with her," Lori said. She had the bucket from our wing. It would work. We had two more buckets from the fifth floor. One girl carried her toiletries in one and one was from the supply closet.

Having Sonja made the next wing go faster. The RA

there was more willing to listen to her than to a group of girls. Like Sonja, she organized her wing.

With each wing that we added, we had more girls to carry more containers of water and more flashlights. We worked our way down to the main floor and the lounge there.

The dorm mother, Kylie, had taken in the desk worker who had fled to the little office behind the main desk. The front doors were locked and all the lights were turned up. Dorm mother always seemed ridiculous for the woman in charge. She was a fifth-year senior, just a bit older than us, and tiny as a bird. Her voice even squeaked but she'd studied education and wasn't afraid to put all of her energy behind her authority when necessary.

Kylie wasn't even a particularly original thinker, staying a bit too close to whatever set of instructions given her, so it was a surprise when she found a couple of spotlights in the storage room near her small apartment.

"This building is old enough, something is always going wrong," she said. "I should phone the other dorm mothers and let them know to rally their RAs to get rid of the creatures in their buildings. Can someone else call campus security so they can work through the campus?"

There were nods. I breathed out. It seemed anticlimactic as if I had been geared up to do more and this was it.

Except it wasn't.

Chapter Twenty-Four

I thought about the handful of campus security people. Even if the police in Havestad worked with them, there weren't enough. Not for the monsters out there. What we needed was a good rainstorm.

"We need to tell the police, too," I said. "And someone post this on your Facebook or something. It seems like news others need to know."

More nods. I saw a couple of people getting out their phones.

"The rest of us can maybe go make sure the quad stays clear," I said.

Kylie had gone to make her phone calls so she wasn't there to override my directives. The other RAs didn't. They were used to, or sort of used to, taking direction from me.

"Maybe we can melt some of the snow?" one of the girls asked.

"How?" I listened with half an ear. It was a good idea.

"We need coats if we're going outside," someone said.

"Let's organize by wings for the groups to get the

coats," I said. The RAs went to work sending various groups up to get coats. When it was our turn, Cassidy and Kennedy grabbed mine for me. It wasn't like I had a door on my room any longer thanks to the monster.

My wingmates tried to get Rebecca to come down, but she wasn't leaving her room. Two of the other RAs texted her. One called.

"She just doesn't believe this is working," Sonja told me. She shrugged as if that was foolish. It probably wasn't as foolish as it seemed to her right at that moment. The creatures were dying because of belief, or not.

I guess, with monsters, seeing was believing.

Once dressed more warmly, we had our water and our lights and we marched outside. Those of us in the front of the line were immediately swarmed by the ugly little creatures with sharp teeth. Water melted the first of them. The lights held the others at bay, though they twittered and screeched at us.

We got a line of people to the door to refill our containers of water.

"Too bad it's winter and the hoses are probably all cleared for the cold," Cassidy said, looking back at the dorm.

I glanced at her. We'd be in trouble if we got the pipes to freeze on the dorms.

"We don't have yard plumbing in the dorms," Sonja said. "Too easy for someone to uncover an outdoor spigot to let pipes freeze as a joke."

"How do they water?" I asked.

"There are sprinklers set around the campus. Maintenance can turn them on. I think there are some outdoor spigots, too."

"There's one over by the cafeteria," Marble said

quickly. "By the water fountain. There's a dog water fountain there, too."

I knew what she was thinking of. I'd seen it, but of course, never paid any attention to it. The water fountain outside was rarely used, particularly since nearly everyone carried their own water bottles now. It was an old fashioned bowl with a little rounded bubbler. It had a heating element on it so that the pipes wouldn't freeze there. Below, there was a foot peddle that would turn on a spigot down below for dogs. Not that dogs were often on campus. It's not like we could have pets, but someone had clearly worried a dog would get thirsty.

"Can we call maintenance and ask them to turn on the sprinklers?" I asked.

Throughout the conversation, we kept passing pans of water and throwing it on the little creatures who gnashed teeth and periodically tried to rush us.

Sonja had already handed off her pan of water and had her phone out. I hadn't even thought to bring mine. I was busy with the little penlight and the pans and bottles and cups of water that I kept tossing at any shadowy thing that moved.

We were a force to be reckoned with, finally.

I should have been terrified of the numbers of the little creatures appearing in the quad around the dorms. I heard a few screams from the other dorms. Someone hadn't been fast enough with the water, perhaps. Other, inhuman screams would echo back. The creatures might get in a bite or a claw but someone was there to save the day.

My shoulder ached where it had been injured, a deep cold ache that made my arm feel heavy. At first, I put it down to all the movement I was doing and the weather. But after a time I had to admit that perhaps there had been something in the claws.

Groans gurgled surrounded us. Then the sprinklers started with a hiss and a spit. I smelled water and mold.

The screams that came from the small creatures on the grass were deafening. In moments there was silence.

I paused looking around at the girls. Everyone was now on the cobbled quad or the walk to the dorm. A few people were damp from the sprinklers. They might get colds but they'd live. The creatures wouldn't.

"Is that it?"

I didn't know who said it.

"For now," I said.

The man I'd seen at the church pushed his way through to me. I smelled lavender and saw the shadow of the ghost who had helped me.

"Do you believe it's done?" he asked quietly.

I breathed in and out. It couldn't be all about me. It had to be about everyone, didn't it?

"If I believe will it be done?" I asked.

"For you."

"Isn't that for everyone?" I didn't understand what he meant. If I believed we had gotten them, it seemed like it had to be over for all people.

"It's about belief," he said again. He was dressed just as he had been at the church. He didn't look any different.

"Who are you?" I asked him.

He smiled at me. "A friend."

I glared.

Naomi gave me a strange look.

"Ask them what they saw in the dorms," he suggested.

"What did you see in the dorms?" I asked Kennedy. "When you threw water on the monster attacking me."

"Didn't you see it?" Kennedy asked. "It was a giant flying monkey. I know you all think I'm obsessed with *The Wizard of Oz* and I guess I am, but I don't know how anyone could see that and not think to throw water on it eventually."

"And the small creatures?" I turned to Cassidy.

"They were the worst right? Like giant spiders or something," she said. She shuddered.

I moved away from that group and asked a few others. Each girl had seen something slightly different. The only reason the water worked was that they all saw it work so they all had the same experience. The monsters themselves had come from our own fears.

I thought about all the horror movies where the heroes think it's over and the monster comes back in a surprise move that was so cliché no one was ever surprised.

Something more was coming.

"It's for you to finish," the man from the church said, having followed along with me as I talked to my dorm mates. He'd been so silent, I'd forgotten he was there. Or maybe he was part of my imagination.

He smiled a bit and bowed.

I rolled my eyes and glanced up at the sky.

"How do I finish?" I asked him.

"You always finish it where it started."

For me, it had started with the fire in the church. We were going to have to go to the old church. I hoped I could get people to follow me.

Chapter Twenty-Five

"I think I need to go to the church," I said. Kennedy and Cassidy had forced their way closer to me. No one mentioned the man I'd been talking to. However, no one had mentioned me having a conversation with the air so there was that. Hopefully, they'd seen him when I'd been talking to him. Maybe some of them even saw him now because I certainly didn't.

"Listen up!" Cassidy called.

Kennedy started talking to people about getting more water in their pans. On the campus, we had the sprinklers. Thank heavens for whoever was manning the maintenance building tonight. They'd been willing to turn on sprinklers in the middle of winter. I'm sure winterizing the pipes probably wasn't cheap, not unless they could take care of it themselves, during the day.

It remained cloudy but whatever snow had been falling earlier had stopped. I walked down towards the far end of the quad, towards the main part of campus. The place didn't seem quite as shadowy as it had but it wasn't exactly friendly. Seeing the sprinklers running when it was that cold out was disorienting. My brain was having a hard time processing whether it was winter or spring.

My body had no such qualms. It was cold. And my shoulder burned and ached. My fingers twitched uncomfortably as if whatever was in the wound made by the claw affected the nerves. It was all belief though. Maybe I could believe I had never been hurt. Or maybe tomorrow I'd wake up and all would be fine.

"It doesn't work like that," my church friend said, appearing beside me.

"Who are you?" I asked.

He just smiled at me, again. I shook my head.

I looked back. Cassidy had a group of people just behind me. Kennedy came hurrying through the group with a backpack full of water bottles. She kept coming until she was walking beside me.

"Just in case," she said. "Not everyone will have turned on sprinklers and there are places where we're not so close to garden areas that won't have sprinklers. Plus, I don't know if they can even run them all at once."

I hadn't ever seen all the sprinklers on at once. They seemed to rotate through, usually early mornings. The old library loomed. Three of the large creatures, which still looked to me like something between human and ape with large tusks. Troll creatures, I thought.

I tossed the pan of water I had over the first one. Cassidy rushed up with a bucket of water and tossed it over them.

The one I'd hit hadn't gotten as much water and though it howled, it kept coming.

Kennedy backed up.

Another girl threw water at it.

The face began to melt. It pounded its chest and

screamed. The sound was abruptly cut off when the water melted through its vocal cords.

The sound echoed through the court and if there were others of its kind coming to its rescue they'd find us soon enough.

Someone flashed around the light. I noticed the wet blackened area further off. Someone had gotten the third creature.

We weren't close to any sprinklers. The maintenance worker had probably used the ones closest to the dorms to help us. This could be a problem.

I paused as empty buckets were passed back through a longer line of women and full ones were passed forward. We needed access to water if we were going to get there.

Someone passed me a large flashlight.

I turned it on, shining it in the darkened shadows around the base of the buildings. Nothing scurried out of the way.

I walked more slowly through this part of the campus. The cobbles under my feet felt good. Buildings loomed on either side. On my left was the old library building, the oldest building at HLC. I'd thought maybe there was something there, but the mysterious man had said I needed to go to the church. Where it started.

Of course, maybe it hadn't started at the church. Maybe it started here. In the old library. Maybe the school was the starting point.

"What do you believe?" a voice whispered, leaving a lingering trace of lavender scent to wrap itself around my nose.

The ghost.

I stopped looking at the building. At the best of times, it was lovely. Tonight, in the dark, it looked ominous enough to be featured in a horror movie. The lights left burning in the windows—the school was going to have a hell of an electric bill—flickered gold. One window was dark, the light probably having burned out from overuse.

The bricks looked dark in the night, and from my angle, the building almost seemed to lean to one side. It was the way the shadows fell but I couldn't get over the sense that I wasn't standing quite straight.

The school had started there. I'd had a sense that this building was important earlier. I'd wanted to research it.

"What's below that building?" I asked someone. I did not want to have to go running through a dark basement to clear out monsters from hell.

"If anything was in the basement, they'd have come out sooner," my ghost whispered to me. At least she wasn't asking me questions that I had to answer in front of people, not like my friend from the church.

That made sense to me. Maybe this wasn't the place.

Except it felt like it was. I walked around to the front, the girls with me following. I turned to look back at the building, at the large double doors that had glass in them now but had once been solid wood. I waited, not sure what I was waiting for.

I glanced upwards towards the rooftop in time to see the shadow of a woman leap off the slanted shingles and fall towards me.

Time slowed as I took in the scene. I heard the sounds of murmurs and gasps behind me. I wasn't the only one who had seen the woman jump.

She was wearing a long dress, or perhaps a nightgown. Her hair was long and fluttered in the wind that her fall generated. She was going to land on her feet, probably breaking her legs. The building was three stories high, plus the attic and part of a basement that came up out of the ground.

Her skirts, if that's what they were, fluttered out around her and she landed easily a few yards away from me. She might have just jumped a few feet rather than three stories. No broken bones for her. Standing beneath the lights of the quad, I noted her pale skin and dark hair. Pits of black greeted me where her eyes should have been. Whether that was from the angle of the lights or that was always how she looked, I didn't know.

"Lussi," someone behind me whispered.

Naturally. I had been reading about Lussi. Someone had to believe in her in the same way they believed in St. Lucia. Too bad they didn't have St. Lucia come to rescue them. They only had me.

Lussi, because that's who this had to be, glided over the cobbles towards me and the small army of women I had with me.

"Submit," she said, pointing a finger at me. Behind her, shadows rose from the cobbles, out of nothing, and became the troll creatures, large and small, that I'd been fighting in the dorm.

To submit to her would mean the death not only of myself but all the girls with me. I knew it deep down. My very DNA believed that truth. If this was about belief, then there would be no rescuing of me or anyone else. Perhaps not the world.

I was no savior, no martyr of the world, but I couldn't go to my death knowing I'd brought everyone else with me. I had to fight on if only to give others the option of life away from this creature.

Kennedy opened one of her bottles of water and sprayed Lussi with it. Water hit her in the face and she turned to glare at Kennedy.

Her skin did not melt. It remained pale as a corpse, which she might just be, buried somewhere deep beneath this old building. Except her legend had started long before the school had been built.

I thought of all the ways I knew to kill supernatural creatures, taken from my reading and watching of horror movies. Destroying the corpse worked, but Lussi wasn't buried there. She was a legend from before white men had taken the land, though she was here, now, for whatever reason.

A smile crossed Lussi's face, showing teeth that seemed too big and slightly pointed. She glided closer.

I didn't see a single step.

I was freezing inside, though I felt sweat on my skin. The fiery ache in my shoulder burned higher, moving down through my chest and across my body.

It took everything I had to stand upright and not double over.

"You can't fight me," Lussi said.

Tell me something I didn't know. I needed help. The ghost had promised helpers when they were needed.

I glanced upward, toward the cloudy sky. A light moved lower and lower, a star falling to the earth.

The surprise I felt must have been mirrored on my face because Lussi also looked up.

Someone tried more water, though that did no more than wet her clothing. Lussi shook it off. It was bright enough now to see the tiny droplets flying everywhere.

The falling star got closer.

I stepped back.

The girls behind me stepped back further.

The light appeared to focus on me.

I needed to move, but my body refused, locked in place.

Lussi began to laugh.

"It's okay," my ghost said.

Fine for her to say. She was already dead. I wanted to live. I'd made that decision earlier. Once again I wanted to scream about the unfairness of it all. I hadn't signed up to do this, didn't have an interest in doing this.

The light hit me.

As it did, I felt as if I'd been dropped into a vat of liquid menthol, the icy hot sensation consuming my entire body, freezing it in a mix of greater pain, but also an odd sense of relief.

The ice burned through the pain in my shoulder so deeply that I gasped. I feared drawing more of the icy hot sensation, but my lungs drew in only air.

I breathed out, watching my breath fog the night air with a silvery fog that glowed long after a normal breath would have dissipated in the chill air.

I felt stronger. My shoulder no longer hurt, though it felt different from the other one. The light around me was stronger.

Gasps of awe came from behind me.

I looked at my hands. They glowed golden.

I was the starlight.

"Not a star," a voice in my head said. This wasn't the ghost. This was something else.

"Take up the sword and fight her," it said.

In my hands was a sword that glowed with light so white it might have been a fluorescent bulb. No heat came from it and I felt no weight.

Maybe it was a sword of my belief.

"Something like that," the voice said.

Lussi had stepped back.

She drew her own sword, similar in nature, though her light glowed gray rather than white.

I wondered if that was because she wasn't completely evil. I mean even I'd watched *Lord of the Rings* and knew about Gandalf the Gray and Gandalf the White. Lussi the Black would be more evil than Lussi the Gray.

"It doesn't work that way," the voice said. "The light is always there, just as darkness is, even if your eyes can't perceive it. Her light comes from believing her cause is just. You *did* destroy her creatures."

Great. I was the bad guy.

"Only in her story. Believe in your own."

The gray sword flew at me. I did what I thought was a parry but it wasn't very good. There was no way I was going to win this fight.

Just as I was about to give up before even starting, something else took over my arms and my body began to work with the sword, parrying Lussi's moves easily. I drove her back. It was darker there, further from the building, but I had my own light, bright enough to keep any of her creatures at bay.

It sounded as if I were locked in a sword battle in the middle of a beehive for all the buzzing I heard. No voices penetrated the buzzing, nor did I hear the sounds of the swords as they hit. I desperately wanted to know if they clanged or thrummed upon meeting each other or made some other sound I hadn't considered.

My body moved of its own volition and the terror I should have had fighting a creature of the dark didn't seem real. I could have been watching a movie where I'd come into the final scenes so late I had no emotional attachment.

The sword cut me down the front and I felt the wetness of blood. That started my heart pumping, but even then, it was detached. A part of me believed I couldn't be defeated, though where that thought had come from, I didn't know.

Another cut, this one on my thigh, sent the same sort of fiery ache I had felt earlier. Despite not being completely in control of my body, I almost went down on one knee. Whatever was doing the fighting saved me from falling, though barely.

Whatever had eased the pain of my shoulder wore off while we fought.

The sword took on weight.

I knew my sword cut and savaged Lussi even more often than she made a hit upon my body. I felt the weight of the weapon trying to cut through her flesh if that's what she was made of. It slowed my movements, made it harder to pull the sword back to me.

My legs began to ache and I feared I couldn't keep going. My body was not made for sword fighting.

I still couldn't hear a thing except for buzzing.

Glancing skyward, the clouds had dissipated though I couldn't have said how they'd moved so quickly. I'd not been fighting for that long.

I wanted to see my dorm mates, to see how they were doing. I couldn't keep going much longer.

I tried to swallow but nothing happened. My tongue stuck to the roof of my mouth and for an instant, I wasn't sure I could get a breath. Then just enough moisture loosened my throat and I gasped in some air.

Lussi smiled at the sounds. She pressed her attack harder.

Whatever was using my body to fight continued on, though I felt my body losing its ability to move the way it needed. Instead of a sword, I might have held an anchor. Swinging became harder.

I nearly let go of the sword when I next hit Lussi. My hands were numb beneath my gloves.

I couldn't feel my nose at all. I didn't remember when I'd stopped feeling it.

The light around me began to brighten.

Lussi glanced up, worried now.

Whatever held the sword pressed the advantage and slammed the glowing bright sword through Lussi's middle, cleaving her in two.

And just like that, Lussi became a liquid shadow that crumpled and broke like a blackened leaf upon being hit with the air.

I couldn't stand a moment longer and fell to one knee. Pink light peeked over the horizon as dawn arrived.

I breathed hard and heavy, wishing for some of the water my dorm mates must have continued to hold, but I had no breath for that, no ability to speak.

Someone came up to me, holding a water bottle. I guzzled some before it was tipped back, taken from me. I wanted to scream, to use that sword against anyone who would stop me from drinking.

Kennedy stepped back, perhaps reading my face.

It was the last thing I saw before everything went black.

Chapter Twenty-Six

The next thing I knew, I was on a gurney with a paramedic looking down at me. He was masked and gloved and covered in heavy clothing. The sky above him was a pale ice blue but the sun was visible and light streamed down on the campus.

The scratch and chill of a plastic mask covered my face. I reached up a hand, but the paramedic guided it down.

"You're injured," he said.

I closed my eyes taking stock of my body. Everything hurt. While I remembered the fight, I didn't quite believe I could have fought all night and survived.

"You didn't fight." I smelled lavender with this comment. The ghost hadn't disappeared with the night.

"Pish. Ghosts don't care about light and dark. I finally got to do something!"

I wondered how dull a life might get if you had to sit in a kitchen all the time and just periodically act out what had gone before.

"It makes sure I remember the important things," my ghost said.

Ghosts who read minds. The mask over my mouth and nose kept me from talking. I heard things besides the buzzing, though I couldn't make out everything. People were talking. A lot of them.

Kennedy came over to the gurney and she smiled at me and nodded. "You did it!"

The gurney was lifted up and into the back of the medic bus. I was going to miss my final. That brought a bit of anxiety and made me toss and turn. The medic with me must have thought I was afraid of the movement because he started whispering calming words to me. I noted the IV in my arm then.

If I felt the needle at all, it was just another ache in my body. I might have climbed a hundred mountains or perhaps competed in back to back all night triathlons the way my body felt. Except for certain places, like the shoulder that felt worse than the rest of me.

My abdominal area burned just like my shoulder. I wanted to look; I remembered the sword slicing me there, the first place Lussi had wounded me. I recalled wetness and the sudden fear that I couldn't keep on fighting, but something else had.

My body might be injured and hurt, but whatever I'd let fight for us had certainly prevailed.

I heard someone say they'd go. I had no idea where. Not long after the bus started on its way to the hospital.

"Just a few minutes to Havestad Emergency Hospital," the medic told me. He still wore a mask and his head was covered with a hat though I saw traces of very dark hair. There were lines at the edges of his eyes. Not a young man then.

"They'll get you set there and assess whether they need

to send you to a bigger hospital and what level they'll need. You have a lot of lacerations, most of which are still leaking blood. You just lie back and let us do the work here, okay?"

I closed my eyes, this time a little more relaxed. I drifted off and came to in a loud room with several nurses and a doctor, at least I think she was a doctor. Things were confused as I drifted in and out of consciousness. They gave me something because I started to feel floaty and my body stopped aching everywhere.

When I woke up, I was in a hospital room attached to several machines. Naomi sat in a chair next to me.

"You're awake," she said, smiling.

"What happened?" I asked.

"Don't you remember?" Naomi set aside the phone she'd been playing with. I noticed a textbook next to her.

"Some." That was good enough. Let her tell me what she knew. That way if I'd gone crazy and attacked the dorm or something I didn't have to admit what I was seeing.

"We cleared the dorm. Do you remember doing that?"

I nodded.

"Then we followed you to the main area outside the old library building. A really pale woman or vampire or something floated down. Kennedy threw water on her but nothing happened. And then a woman with light around her head fell and landed inside you. You started fighting the pale woman with a sword and kept on almost all night. When the sun just started over the horizon, you cut through her middle and she dissolved into dust. A breeze came up and scattered the ashes." Naomi's eyes were big and she talked quickly, trying to spit everything out, lest I correct her or something.

"After that, you fell down on your knees like you

couldn't stand anymore. You were bleeding all over. Kennedy and I tried to get bandages and stuff and give you water while Cassidy called 911. This woman in a white robe with a red sash and wreath on her head with a large candle, leaned down and fed you a small wafer and said thank-you."

I didn't remember any of that last part.

"I remember the fight and falling down. I think I remember the water," I said quietly. "I don't remember the woman in white."

"She was there. It's funny. When we started comparing notes we all saw the monsters differently, but when we saw the pale woman, we all saw her pretty much the same. I mean there were some differences, but that's just the stuff that everyone argues about like how pale she was and the shape of her eyes. And, we all saw the woman in white. I think it was St. Lucia and she took over your body for the fight. It kind of fits."

"I thought St. Lucia was about leadership, strength of character, and compassion. That's not exactly me." My shoulder throbbed again. Whatever the woman in white had given me, it wasn't enough to get rid of all my aches and pains.

"Who got us all together and started clearing the dorm?" Naomi stood up, hands on her hips. "And who just kept putting herself in front of monsters?"

"Someone else would have done it if I hadn't." I mean, yeah, it seemed like something was pushing me into the role, but it's not like someone else couldn't have played the role. I just had a feeling I had to die for that mantle to fall on someone else.

Naomi shook her head. "Own your power, woman!" Then she smiled and giggled sitting back down.

I closed my eyes and tried to go back to sleep. It hit me then that I'd probably missed my last final.

"I missed my final, didn't I?" I said.

"We made sure your professor knew why," Naomi said. "You have a pass until next semester, at least. I think the whole school knows what you did, not just for us, but probably the world."

Great. Someone made me a folk hero. I went from one of the dealers who ruined Lucia Bride in Dubuque to the anointed of St. Lucia herself in Havestad. Clearly, Lucia needed better information on who she was choosing, because I was so not in line as an example of who she was.

I must have drifted off because when I opened my eyes, Naomi wasn't there but the woman in white stood nearby. She didn't have a red sash tied at the waist. To me, it looked brown. Her hair was light brown and pulled up in a braid that circled her head.

No candles graced her head. She sat on the side of my bed. It didn't seem like a dream. I smelled a faint scent of pine and something that reminded me of early morning. The mattress sank down where she sat, just a little, the way it would for a real person.

The woman in white smiled at me. "You are my choice for all the reasons Naomi gave. Not a one of us is perfect. It's only when we're tested by the darkness that our true natures come out. You were willing to put yourself in harm's way because it seemed to you that to not do that would cause the suffering of millions. That's what my legacy is about."

"I only did it because I knew I'd die anyway," I said.

Lucia smiled. She patted the side of my face. "I can't do anything about your shoulder. That comes from not quite believing the creature would be destroyed by water. Your muscles should feel normal by tomorrow, though.

And your doctors will be shocked at how fast your other wounds are healing."

"Am I going to die from the shoulder wound?" I asked. I imagined a long, drawn-out death, becoming weaker and weaker, unable to function.

"No. It will just pain you from time to time. To remind you of the importance of having faith."

"But it wasn't faith in God," I said.

"But it was faith in something, wasn't it?" Lucia said. "You think it was faith in yourself, but you listened to a ghost and to a man who wasn't there. You've seen the queen of the dark and you've seen me. Tell me you can't believe in God, even if he doesn't conform to the images you've learned in your church."

She was right. I did sort of have to believe in something.

"Believe in the goodness of whatever face of God appeals to you. And to the best of your ability, live up to those ideals."

"Why now? Why here?" I whispered. If I had to be pushed to do things I'd never have believed I could, or perhaps, if Lucia was right, I did believe I could, then why had it happened?

"The church fire. It was an accident, electrical, though there was some gasoline stored down below for the lawn mower. On the far side is a low ramp that allowed them to store the groundskeeping equipment. The pastor fell down the stairs to the basement making sure no one was there. Everyone thought he'd gotten out. He believed that dying in the church in a fire on a night that signals the beginning of the darkest nights of the year would unleash the creatures of evil. And so they came. Until you stopped them."

I watched as she drifted out of the room. I felt very

tired then and closed my eyes. When I woke up again, Kennedy had replaced Naomi in the chair.

"Your parents are here," she said. "They went out to get some dinner."

I couldn't believe that quiet Kennedy was practically my right-hand person. And a believer.

"Thanks," I said. "They're probably pretty upset."

"They've heard what you did. And given how quiet tonight is, even if it isn't yet Yule, pretty much everyone is convinced you stopped the invasion. And I think belief is the most important part, don't you?"

"I do," I said. I wondered if Kennedy had her own ghost talking to her. I sniffed the air but got no trace of lavender. It was too bad, I'd have liked to thank her. Maybe when I came back to school after the holiday, I could leave a sprig of lavender in the kitchen. I had a suspicion she'd like that.

On cue, my parents entered and Kennedy slipped out, leaving me to their ministrations and the logistics of getting me home. I laid back and let them take care of me instead of resisting everything they wanted to do for me. It was their way of showing they cared. I was going to break their hearts when I struck out on my own, but if I'd learned nothing else in all of this, I learned that running a property management company wasn't for me.

I wasn't quite sure what was, but I knew it dealt with law. I'd spend next semester figuring out where I fit. But first, I had Christmas at home and I still had some shopping to do once I got there, though given my mom's fussing, that might all have to be done online. Still, it would all work out.

Things always did.

About Bonnie Elizabeth General

Bonnie Elizabeth could never decide what to do, so she wrote stories about amazing things and sometimes she even finished them.

While rejection stung her so badly in person, she spent most of her young life talking to cats and dogs rather than people, she was unusually resilient when it came to rejections on her writing, racking up a good number of them.

Floating through a variety of jobs, including veterinary receptionist, cemetery administrator, and finally acupuncturist, she continued to write stories.

When the internet came along (yes she's old), she started blogging as her cat, because we all know cats don't notice rejection. Then she started publishing.

Bonnie writes in a variety of genres. Her popular Whisper series is contemporary fantasy and her Teenage Fairy Godmother series is written for teens. She has been published in a number of anthologies and is working on expanding her writing repertoire.

She lives with her husband (who talks less than she does) and her three cats, who always talk back.

Stay in Touch

Also by Bonnie Elizabeth

The Frost Witch Saga

October Snow

November Frost

December Storm

Appalachian Souls

Souls Lost

Souls Broken

The Ash Jericho Series

An Inheritance to Die For

A Discovery to Die For

A Distraction to Die For

The Whisper Novels

Whisper Bound

Taken by the Sound

An Air of Suspicion

Little Dog Lost

Death Interrupted

Down in Whisper

A Haunting Whisper

A Haunting Attraction

Secrets Not Whispers

Only Human

Other Novels

One Bad Wish

Sun Spot Magic

Ghosts from the Past

Unnatural Secrets

Find them all at your favorite bookseller or check us out at
MyBigFatOrangeCat.com